THE FORTUNES OF JACKY

THE
FORTUNES OF
JACKY

by

KATHARINE L. OLDMEADOW

THE CHILDREN'S PRESS
LONDON AND GLASGOW

Printed and Made in Great Britain

CONTENTS

CHAPTER I

ONE fine spring day a rather unusual procession wound its way along the road which leads to the south coast of England.

Village children playing outside cottage doors at first sight had high hopes it might turn out to be a circus procession, because it was led by two pretty girls riding white ponies. But their plain, purple frocks belted with white and their bare heads did not in the least resemble the sweeping skirts and gaily plumed headgear of the ladies of the Ring. Following the riders came a caravan driven by a man who might easily have been a gipsy or travelling showman. He was burnt almost black by the sun and his clothes were scanty, comfortable and decidedly shabby; but surely no gipsy or showman would declaim aloud Shelley's ode, *To a Skylark*, so passionately into the ears of his horse as this gentleman was doing at the particular moment this story begins.

The caravan was of the Romany type, painted green, and through the open door one could see a fascinating array of bright pots and pans and over the door painted in white letters was the name: Travellers' Joy.

A smallish girl wearing a rose-pink frock belted with white and a rose-pink sun-bonnet sat on the steps of the caravan with her lap full of bluebells and the big, dappled mare that drew the caravan wore garlands of spring flowers. Next came ten school-girls of all ages and sizes riding bicycles. The older ones wore purple frocks with collars and belts of white; the middle-aged ones were in dark blue and white and the youngest wore green, with the same touch of white as their companions. Three ladies, all riding bicycles, followed the schoolgirls, wearing light tweeds, cool blouses, and small, sensible hats. The little rough-haired terrier rushing along in such deli-rious joy was a member of the party and upon his brand new green collar was written, *Christopher Col-umbus, Rainbow End, Broomy Hill, Dorset*, and like his namesake he certainly looked as if he was out for great adventures.

The bicycles were decorated with primroses and bluebells and there was an air of gaiety about the travellers which made all who beheld them feel gay and youthful too.

All these young people were the pupils of Mrs. Bly, who had left her school in London in the care of her partner and was now trekking southwards in order to have an open-air school during the summer months.

Mrs. Bly, the tallest and prettiest of the three ladies, was not only very learned, but very charming and had delightful ideas about bringing up young people though she was sometimes called a crank. Like the old Spartan law-makers she firmly believed that hard, physical training should be given to girls, and she was convinced that the women of ancient Greece were sweet-tempered, clear-minded, and famed for their beauty, courage, and intellect because they were made physically fit by racing, wrestling, swimming, throwing the javelin, and practising other exercises in the open air.

London, however, is not a good place for wrestling and javelin-throwing, especially in the costume prescribed by Spartan law, and though the school left by Mrs. Bly was not very far from Hampstead the pond there is not really suitable for girls to swim in and Mrs. Bly could not afford to make a private swimming pool. Indeed, the only reason she had begun her school in the old town house was because it belonged to Mr. Bly, the little man who was driving the caravan and reciting Shelley's *Ode to Griselda,* the dappled mare.

Mr. Bly was a most useful husband for a schoolmistress, not only because he owned a house large enough for a school and was himself as docile and obedient as the very smallest of his wife's pupils; but because he was a professor of English literature as well as a very learned naturalist and botanist and was able to teach these subjects to the girls.

Mrs. Bly had always wanted to have a school in the country, and the Professor, as a naturalist, longed for an out-door life, so when, while on a holiday, they came across a piece of land for sale on the Dorset coast they decided to buy it and use it as a summer school for girls needing sunshine and an out-door life. The land had already been used as a training-camp and the wooden huts erected upon it were quite large enough for themselves and their pupils.

Unconventional parents approved of the plan and were willing that the last week of the Easter holidays should be spent in travelling to the new school by road.

The pupils themselves were more than content at

the prospect of spending the summer term in tents and huts at a place delightfully called Rainbow End.

They had travelled the first stage by train to the village where the caravan and Griselda awaited them, and then they had taken to the road, halting at country towns for the night. Those that could not be accommodated at the inn were billeted cosily in cottages, and though some of these cottages provided feather beds which were perhaps a little too cosy, and others offered flock mattresses so lumpy they could never have suited a real princess, nobody minded, nobody grumbled, and everyone slept like tops.

The lady who rode beside Mrs. Bly was Miss Lyle, a very learned and capable person worth three ordinary teachers and perhaps rather wasted on a small camp-school; but she needed a rest; loved educational experiments, and was an old friend of the headmistress. The third lady, Miss Carroll, a young girl with short hair and long limbs, was the games mistress and knew all there was to be known about eurhythmics and folk-dancing. She meant to do her duty and have a good time, too, at Rainbow End.

The two girls riding ahead of the procession were Cecilia Corble and Audrey Gibbs and they were lucky enough to be the owners of the ponies they were riding.

The little girl in the caravan wearing the pink sunbonnet was Felicity, Mrs. Bly's only child. She was the owner of Christopher Columbus, and a cat, now slumbering in the caravan, who was called Cato.

The schoolgirls on the bicycles were of all ages, sizes, and dispositions and what some of them did, and why they did it, will all be told in this story.

CHAPTER II

ENTER JACINTHA

THE Professor had just finished reciting Shelley's ode into Griselda's patient ears when Ethel Forbes gave a shriek and tumbled off her bicycle. Everyone else tumbled off theirs too, and the caravan came to a standstill because this particular shriek meant that Ethel had another fly in her eye and a halt must be called while somebody rendered first-aid. Ethel's eyes attracted flies as surely as a honey-pot. Geraldine Monk said it was because they were so round and prominent that it was natural for any fly seeking some convenient place to commit suicide to mistake them for watery, round ponds, and whenever such a tragedy occurred Ethel fell off her bicycle with a shriek and showed no resemblance at all to a courageous Greek maiden while the victim was being extracted.

"There!" said Mrs. Bly. "It's out! What a huge beast! We must get you some goggles, Ethel, if you continue to be so attractive to these horrid insects."

"I always knew these midges would spoil everything," moaned Ethel. "And that one was so enormous and hurt so frightfully I don't believe it was a midge at all."

Immediately, the Professor, who had left the caravan to help with the operation, disinterred the victim's corpse from the corner of Ethel's handkerchief and examined it for identification.

"You are right, child," he said amiably. "It is a specimen of the common house-fly. When *I* was a boy we were cautioned in prose and verse never to hurt such a harmless creature, but now, I believe, young people are given so much a head for their dead bodies."

"Well then, Ethel ought to make her fortune!" cried Geraldine, and immediately all the girls began to chant the health-slogan of the house-fly;

> *I visit every rubbish-heap,*
> *I never wash my feet,*
> *And every single chance I get*
> *I walk on what you eat.*

"Well, I don't care if they do, I'd love to be a fly," said Felicity, who had joined the party. "Fancy being clever enough to walk upside down on the ceiling."

"My pet," said her father, remembering he was a schoolmaster whose duty was to instruct, "if you had suckers on the soles of your feet as the fly has, *you* could enjoy a walk on the ceiling; but Shakespeare would never have approved of your slogan, girls, and this is how he addressed a fly killer:

> *Out on thee, murderer!*
> *How if that fly had a father or mother?*
> *How would he hang his slender, gilded wings,*
> *And buzz lamenting in the air?*
> *Poor harmless fly!*

" Poor harmless fly, indeed!" cried Mrs. Bly. " I wonder how many of Shakespeare's friends and relatives *he* murdered by walking on their food after visiting medieval rubbish-heaps? Now Ethel, pull the brim of your hat well down, perhaps that will keep these innocent creatures out of your eyes. We must go on now, or we shall never reach Rainbow End before tea."

" There's a donkey-cart coming, Professor, and Griselda's taking up all the road," called out Miss Carroll, and everyone turned to watch the approaching traveller. She was a girl of about fourteen, very thin, and with a short crop of reddish hair which looked gold in the sunshine.

She wore a skimpy and washed-out blue cotton frock and sandals on her bare feet and there was something very determined in the way she drove the donkey-cart.

She was sitting on an old leather suit-case and leaning against it was a portfolio. In the cart behind there was a hen-coop containing six hens.

" What an extraordinary-looking child!" exclaimed Miss Lyle.

" But don't stare at her like that, girls," ordered Mrs. Bly. " And do get Griselda moving, Jim."

The Professor's name was Jim, and he was often referred to as " Sunny Jim " by his pupils.

As soon as the procession was on the move again the girl in the donkey-cart held up her hand and cried out, " Oh, do wait, please," and she began to urge on the donkey.

Very much puzzled the party halted and Mrs. Bly

went back a few steps, for it was evident the girl wanted to speak to her.

" Are you the schoolmistress, please?"

" Yes, I'm Mrs. Bly."

Every girl pricked up her ears and drew a little nearer, for there was a feeling that something unusual was about to happen.

" Would you mind telling me how much it costs to come to your school?"

" How much it *costs*?" Mrs. Bly was annoyed, but not so annoyed as most headmistresses would be at being held up by a shabby girl in a donkey-cart with a demand to be told how much she charged her pupils for the benefit of a rather unusual but excellent education.

" Yes—if your school is not too dear I'd like to come to it awfully; but Dick says he'll bet a fiver the fees would ruin a duke's daughter."

As a matter of fact Mrs. Bly's school fees were rather high, though there were no duke's daughters in the procession; but she much resented this Dick—whoever he was—making bets about her and could not help saying rather coldly: " Really—and might one ask who is Dick and why do you want to place yourself in my school in such a hurried and extraordinary manner?"

The girls pressed a little nearer, hoping Mrs. Bly would not order them to go on while she dealt with this amazing young person, and indeed she did ask Miss Carroll to move forward with her charges, but Ethel (whose besetting sin was curiosity) showed immense resource by attracting another fly into her eye and while Miss Lyle was removing it her schoolfellows were able to enjoy the rest of the conversation.

" Dick is my step-father. He's got a chance of a job out in Kenya at once if only he can get rid of me. We've asked about lots of schools, but they all want to be paid in advance, which is jolly awkward when you haven't got a bean. Then yesterday, some-one turned up and offered to take our cottage fur-nished for a year and Dick decided I would have to go to the Vicarage and share their governess, which I'd simply *loathe*. Last night I saw you all putting up in the village and somebody told me about your camp-school. I thought it sounded awfully jolly and rushed to tell Dick, but he said he bet you would be too expensive, too."

" But why didn't your step-father come and see me at the inn, last night?"

" He wouldn't face it . . . he's like that. He said it was no good and I should just have to put up with the Vicarage. But this morning he went off to town to see about his kit so I just packed up my things and did a bunk. The man who has taken our cottage saw my Japanese prints and says they are worth a good bit—so I brought them along, too, and thought perhaps you wouldn't mind having them instead of money."

At this extraordinary suggestion Mrs. Bly gasped and the listening girls simply hugged themselves with joy and hoped with all their hearts that this strange girl *would* be their schoolfellow.

" Of course I know people don't pay school-bills with pictures and hens and if you don't like the idea I must go back, of course; but I left a note for Dick saying that if I wasn't there when he came back he would know I'd fixed it."

" But my dear child . . . surely you know that it is impossible for me to accept a new pupil in this sudden way. I do not even know your name?"

" It's Jacintha Drew, and my step-father's name is Richard Erly and we live at Flagstones, a cottage about two miles from here."

" And where is your mother?"

" She's been dead five years, and my father died when I was two. I haven't a single relation in the world that I know about and I was left on Dick's hands which was jolly rough on him. He is awfully decent about it though, and we've pulled along somehow. We have been frightfully down on our luck lately and Dick says if he had known about the Japanese prints he would have sold them ages ago."

" Then it is a good thing he didn't know," said Miss Lyle, joining in briskly. She guessed shrewdly that Mr. Richard Erly was not a very satisfactory step-father.

" Beatrice!" shouted the Professor to his wife, " why are we not moving?"

" Of course if I were in your place I should not hesitate one moment," continued Miss Lyle. " I should take the child along—hens, pictures, and all."

" I couldn't do that without first seeing her step-father," said Mrs. Bly firmly, and she added in an undertone, " After all, one doesn't pick up one's pupils by the roadside."

" And such awful things happen nowadays," said Miss Carroll, who had drawn near, and Jacintha, hearing this remark, said coolly:

" I'm not a thief, or anything of that sort . . . if I were they wouldn't have had me at the Vicarage."

The Vicarage certainly made a respectable background for this strange girl and Mrs. Bly said kindly: " I'm afraid the only thing I can do, Jacintha, is to come back with you and see your step-father."

" But he isn't there."

" Then I must see the Vicar."

" He lives seven miles away from here. I say— what's *wrong* with me?"

The girl seemed unable to understand this suspicious attitude and there was a hurt, wistful tone in her voice which touched Mrs. Bly's heart.

" Nothing is wrong with you, Jacintha," she said in her kind, sensible way; " but all this is very unusual, you know, and I must consult my husband about it."

Mrs. Bly managed her husband, her child, her school and her household successfully all by herself; but there were occasions when she liked to say, " I must consult my husband."

If things went wrong afterwards it was comforting to put some of the blame on his amiable shoulders.

She made her way to the caravan and told him Jacintha's tragic tale.

" I don't know what we can do," she said unhappily.

" *Do!* Bless my soul, Beatrice, you really can't think of returning this child to a brute of a fellow who evidently doesn't care what becomes of her? Bring her along, of course, and make inquiries to-morrow of this Vicar chap."

" But she has not got a certificate of health and

might be sickening for mumps or measles this minute. I hate to be fussy, you know that, Jim, but I must think of the girls and be conventional sometimes.''

'' She won't give 'em measles in the open air, and you can put her in a tent to sleep until you find out about her. Now, for goodness' sake let's move on, my dear.''

'' Yes, we will, Jim.'' Mrs. Bly turned back to the donkey-cart where Jacintha sat, seemingly quite unconscious of the many curious eyes watching her.

'' Well, Jacintha . . . the Professor suggests that you come along with us now and that we find out all about your step-father's plans to-morrow.''

'' How kind of you!'' Jacintha gave her a beaming smile. '' I'm awfully keen on the way you do things, you know.''

'' What a calm, patronising young person,'' remarked Miss Lyle, and Mrs. Bly said quite seriously, '' And I hope we shall like the way *you* do things too, Jacintha. Listen, girls, this is Jacintha Drew and she is coming to spend the night with us at Rainbow End and may stay with us altogether.''

Every girl flashed a smile at the newcomer, though Ethel Forbes whispered audibly, '' Dear me . . . what *next*, I wonder? Who *is* she, I'd like to know?'' and to her discomfiture Jacintha answered calmly, '' Nobody in particular, though my mother's great-great-great-uncle was beheaded on Tower Hill for loyalty to King Charles.''

'' Never mind your ancestors now, child,'' said Mrs. Bly. '' Now girls, all mount, please, and let us get on.''

'' Well, just fancy her attacking me like that,'' said

Ethel indignantly to her companions. "And I never knew people before who bragged about relatives who were executed."

"It depends on *how* they were executed," explained Joanna Treherne. "If they were beheaded hundreds of years ago it *is* something to swank about."

"And I wasn't bragging," said Jacintha, hearing again with uncanny swiftness. "She asked me who I was and I tried to tell her."

"Don't crowd and chatter, girls," sang out Miss Carroll. "Keep in twos, and move more quickly, please."

The travellers began to move southwards again until they came to the rolling downs ablaze with gorse and painted with the bright colours of downland flowers which are so small, so lovely, and so much brighter than the flowers of the woods.

The Professor drew up Griselda, took off his hat and addressed the party solemnly. "My friends, let us pay tribute to one of the most beautiful sights in the world. When the great Linnaeus saw gorse in full bloom for the first time, he went down on his knees and thanked God he had been given eyes to see such beauty."

The girls all sniffed rapturously, and Georgie Kent said, unpoetically, but truly, "It's a gorgeous scent, just like warm raspberry jam." And then she gave a jump, for the donkey-cart had rattled up and Jacintha was prodding her with a stick and saying, "Would you mind telling me who was 'the great Linnaeus'?"

"I don't know. I'm not clever, only bright and

beautiful," answered Georgie. " Ethel, go and ask Joanna who the great Linnaeus was—she's simply stuffed with general information."

But Joanna did not know and neither did any of the girls near enough to be asked, but Miss Carroll, hearing the question, sent Ethel back with the news that " the great Linnaeus " was a great botanist and it was disgraceful none of them knew it.

" And how on earth are we to know things we have not been told?" asked Georgie. " That's the worst of clever people, they are so horribly superior. Are you clever?" she asked Jacintha.

" I'm clever at getting my own way—at least that is what Dick says, and I know lots of things you don't learn at school. I suppose it's because I've knocked about the world a bit," Jacintha answered calmly.

" Where have you been?" inquired Ethel, hoping the new girl had never been farther than Scotland, which was the extent of her own travels.

" Oh, we roughed it in Canada for a year—and I've been up and down Scotland, England and Wales and once . . ."

" Girls!" cried Mrs. Bly. " You see that hill in front of us? When we reach the top we shall be exactly on the spot where we stood and first saw Rainbow End and I christened it. It was just after a shower of rain and the end of the loveliest rainbow I ever saw dipped into that belt of pine trees."

" Where the rainbow ends as I've been told,
Lies treasure hid in a crock of gold!"

chanted Felicity. " Oh, Father . . . shall we really find a treasure?"

" My pet," said the Professor solemnly, " if we all don't come home at the end of six months with the greatest treasure on earth, I'm a Dutchman!"

CHAPTER III

LOB'S SCOUSE

THE huts that were to shelter the little company for the summer months were more picturesque than most of these wooden buildings.

They nestled cosily under a shoulder of the downs with their doors and windows facing southwards to the sea and were protected on the north and east by a thick belt of pine-trees.

They had recently been occupied by ladies studying for a horticultural career and they had left many charming little touches.

The huts were raised on wooden piles and each one had a covered verandah reached by a flight of steps and over the wooden pillars climbed honeysuckle. Behind the huts the downs rose in green terraces and the effect, combined with the bright sunlight and white goats tethered here and there with their little fawn-coloured kids, made the settlement look almost like a Swiss mountain village and enchanting to the travellers looking down on it from the hilltop.

There were three large huts; each one separated from the other by a narrow strip of cultivated land, good brown earth patterned with emerald ribbons of fast-growing seeds. Short, turfy grass stretched before the huts and below, the ground sloped to a broad, green plateau and grassy cliffs. Rough wooden steps led down to a golden stretch of sands where stood four bathing-huts gaily painted in stripes of white and green.

There was not a house to be seen for miles and it all seemed so lonely and deserted that Felicity exclaimed, " If only there were some banana and coconut trees it would be almost as nice as a desert island."

" Well—it's Rainbow End, at last, girls," said Mrs. Bly, but before the cheers had subsided Miss Lyle remarked, " Who on earth is that person sitting like Patience on a monument in the middle of what I suppose must be called our playing-field?"

" It's not a monument, it's a tin box," announced the literal Georgie, and Mrs. Bly began to look alarmed. " Surely it can't be Miss Pratt? I told her to arrive early to-day and have everything in order and a hot supper prepared for us."

Mrs. Bly had no intention of allowing her pupils to spend too much of their time on domestic work.

" Let them learn to cook and wash up in a real holiday camp by all means," she argued. " But here other things are more important. An open-air life need not be a perpetual picnic and would be bad for all our manners. Besides, just because I'm living a camp life I don't propose to eat all sorts of picnic messes, so we will take a good cook with us and a domestic help too, to do the work."

But the helpers in Mrs. Bly's London home refused

to camp out in the country and the advice from kind friends was to get two strong country girls from the nearest village.

This advice Mrs. Bly could not take because she wanted to give two town-dwellers the benefit of sea breezes and she searched until she found a cook who suffered from nerves and, according to herself, "hankered after the seaside."

An anæmic-looking young Cockney also expressed a great desire for country life and she, too, was engaged and instructed to reach Rainbow End and make preparations for the travellers.

" I don't see any smoke coming out of the chimneys, Mother," said Felicity, who was a remarkably observant child.

" No, there isn't any smoke. I don't like that. Oh dear me, I do hope nothing has gone wrong. Now girls—*don't* rush—we will arrive in an orderly way, if you please."

" The animals went in two by two," quoted Geraldine aside. " Well, I shan't mind how long I live in such a jolly-looking ark so long as it doesn't rain."

As the party slipped through the sandy lane which led to the camp the waiting figure on the box could no longer be seen but the thought of her quite spoilt Mrs. Bly's pleasure in the arrival. She felt somehow convinced that it *was* Miss Pratt and that for some reason she no longer " hankered after the seaside."

No sooner had the caravan arrived followed by riders, bicyclists and Jacintha's donkey chariot than her worst fears were realised.

It was Miss Pratt sitting on a monument, which was a bright yellow tin box. She was fashionably dressed and wore the pained and martyred expression of a very much ill-used person.

"I'll drive Griselda straight to that sunny corner and fix her up, my love," said the Professor hastily. Domestic science did not interest him and he had never wanted to study the habits of cooks; indeed he considered the common house-fly a more interesting creature and less annoying.

"Well, Miss Pratt," said Mrs. Bly brightly. "How are you this lovely day and where is Doris?"

"I'm not as I should be, madam—and Doris is in one of those summer-houses changing." She looked contemptuously towards the principal hut.

"And why are you sitting out here—isn't it too hot for you?"

"No, madam—I'm never one to go off without a word, and I'd like to say at once, madam, that I'm sitting here waiting for the taxi to take me to the station."

"To the station? But why?"

"You said it was the seaside, madam."

"Well, so it is." Mrs. Bly looked at the vast deep stretching before them. Surely Miss Pratt could not demand more sea than that, or more " side " than the miles of yellow sands.

"Not the sort I've been used to, madam. Where's the pier and the people? Where's the boarding-'ouses and the shops with the picture postcards?" The martyr's voice became shrill and in her excitement she lost her " h's " as well as her temper.

"But surely you can do without things of that sort?" cried Mrs. Bly, and Miss Lyle murmured, " Poor creature! She *is* in a bad way," while the girls flung themselves down on the grass and wickedly enjoyed the situation.

"Excuse me, miss . . . but I'm not ashamed of liking a bit of life around me, and I should never sleep a wink so near that wood. It's just the sort of place to 'arbour murdering tramps and I see there's only one gentleman here to protect us and he don't look over-strong. I'd go potty in this place, indeed I would, madam."

"Nonsense! The fresh air and quiet will do your nerves good. Take off your hat and try it for a week and see."

"There's another thing too, madam. I could never work with oil. I felt sure you'd have gas-stoves and everything convenient to hand. My nerves would never stand getting the bath water hot with oil."

"But my dear woman, we don't expect you to get the sea hot and that is where we intend to bathe!" Miss Lyle joined in briskly. "Now do be sensible, and I can assure you you will not regret it."

"If you will excuse me, ladies, I'd be obliged if you'd let me go without any more arguments as I'm beginning to come over queer. I gave the lad that brought the groceries sixpence to order a taxi for me, and I can hear it coming now." Miss Pratt gave a deep sigh as a taxi-horn was heard tooting in the distance.

"I think you are treating me very badly," said Mrs. Bly severely, and Miss Pratt shouted shrilly, "And what about the way *I've* been treated—brought out to a place that gives me the 'orrors? There's some that would ask for . . ."

" There, that will do," said Mrs. Bly quietly.
" Here's your car . . . go at once, please."

The taxi-man flung the tin box aboard and with a
disdainful glance at the company one of the treasures
Mrs. Bly had hoped to find at Rainbow End vanished
for ever.

" And a jolly good riddance, too, I should say,"
remarked Geraldine, not realising that with Miss Pratt
went the hope of a good evening meal.

Mrs. Bly was a placid person and seldom lost her
temper, but now she felt decidedly ruffled and angry.
She was responsible for the well-being of nearly
twenty tired, hungry people who had been six days
on the road where meals had been mostly of a picnic
description. Learned as she and Miss Lyle were they
did not include cooking among their accomplishments
and Miss Carroll, too, was more ornamental than
useful from a domesticated point of view.

" Well, girls," she said quietly, " we must make
the best of it and perhaps Doris can do something for
us. I wonder where she is?"

At that moment the door of the largest hut opened
and Doris, looking exactly like a parlour-maid on
the stage, came tripping out. She wore a very smart
black frock, light stockings, and high-heeled shoes. A
wisp of muslin and lace tied round her waist was
plainly intended for an apron. On her pale little
Cockney face there was such a delighted grin that her
new mistress felt cheered. It looked as though the
place had not yet given Doris the " 'orrors."

" Good-afternoon, Doris. You are not going to
desert us, I hope?"

" Not me, ma'am," replied Doris, beaming.

"This place is a fair treat and I told her so—but if you ask me she's dotty already and best out of the road. Them daisies look all right, don't they, ma'am, and there's a sparrer singing in them yellow bushes something beautiful. Listen! It's at it again!"

The golden notes of a nightingale in full song chimed from the gorse bushes and Cecilia cried, "Oh, I say . . . it's a nightingale!"

One of the girls tittered to hear Doris compare the sweetest singer in the world to a twittering sparrow, but Doris was not offended.

"Nightingale!" she cried. "Well I never! I've heard it on the wireless but it sounded more squeaky-like. Isn't it pretty-like, ma'am?"

Mrs. Bly began to cheer up more than ever. If this little Cockney who had never heard anything but the roar of London traffic was thrilled by the nightingale's golden flute, it looked as if she would settle down cosily near nature's heart.

"It is pretty, Doris, and I'm so glad you seem happy here. Now the question is what can we do about a hot meal for everybody?"

"It's a real dirty trick her going off like this, ma'am, and if you ask me the meat's going off, too. I don't say it's bad, mind, but it's just asking to be cooked and that grocer never sent us a drop of oil and she never noticed it."

"Then we must have eggs cooked over a spirit lamp. It won't hurt us."

"Eggs *again*," murmured Ethel Forbes. "We had them for breakfast and lunch. Mummy said she was afraid of this and it would all be too happy-go-lucky."

"I must say, I'm sick of scrap meals myself," said

Sally Parker and Geraldine added rather tartly, "I'd rather they were scrappy than raw like this meat they are discussing. After all, we are not camping in caves."

"Don't grumble, girls," advised Georgie. "What does it matter what we eat in this gorgeous place? I'm longing to see our billets. I say, do look at that girl! She's chummed up with Sunny Jim pretty quickly."

Jacintha certainly seemed to have made friends with the amiable Professor while they had both been un-harnessing their steeds and now Griselda, Slowboy, the donkey and the two ponies were happily sampling the sweet, short turf quite independent of cooks and oil-stoves.

"What a pity we can't all solve the food question so easily," sighed Mrs. Bly. "Jim . . . have you heard the news? Miss Pratt has gone! She says it isn't a real seaside with no picture post-cards. Doris is a gem, but she can't cook, and instead of the Irish stew I planned for supper we must have eggs and cocoa again. To-morrow I'll go in search of another cook."

"If you find a cook in this place, my love, I shall be extremely surprised," prophesied the Professor. "And if I go on eating eggs I shall become aware I have a liver and probably beat my wife and child as well as my pupils. Why on earth is that girl dressed up like that? It looks most ridiculous in a place of this sort."

"Never mind, dear. We must be tactful and get her to dress suitably by degrees. She's such a sweet girl and devoted to daisies and sparrows and nightingales. Now, girls . . . please don't make all this noise. We haven't come here to live like savages. Yes, of course you may explore the huts. What is it Jacintha?"

Jacintha stood by her looking much happier. "It's just this," she said eagerly, "if you don't want me to be in the school and I can see you are not really keen on it . . . why can't *I* be the cook?"

"Now, Jacintha, you really must not hinder me. I've so much to do I simply can't have my time wasted."

"But please, I'm trying to save time. You said you wanted to have a hot meal to-night, so why can't I cook it?"

"Might one ask where and when you have cooked?"

"Everywhere—and at all times. Why, I roughed it out west for a year with Dick."

Mrs. Bly began to wonder if she had been mistaken in thinking herself unconventional and different from most headmistresses, because, somehow, she was not sure if she wanted a girl in her school who had "roughed it out west."

"The question seems to be, can Jacintha cook or can she not?" said the Professor. "And the best way to settle it, Beatrice, is to let her try and then we shall know."

"There is no oil, you know, Jacintha. We can manage to make tea on the spirit-stoves but everything else will have to be cooked in some primitive way which I suppose we should all have learnt before we came."

"I can manage without oil," insisted Jacintha undaunted

"Very well, if you can cook a hot meal for nineteen

F.O.J.   B

people in time for supper I shall think you a wonderful person, Jacintha.''

"And while you do it I'll run up a billet for those blessed hens of yours; for if you fail and we have to live on eggs we must encourage the birds to make themselves at home.'' The Professor escaped.

"Do you want anyone to help you, Jacintha?''

"I thought too many cooks spoilt the broth,'' objected Sally Parker who was dying to explore the camp and had no wish to be commandeered.

"Oh, *do* choose me,'' cried Felicity. "I do so want to learn to cook with nothing most awfully.''

"No, Felicity,'' said her mother. "You must attend to your poor little cat. You *would* bring him and he hasn't enjoyed being shut up at all. Take him out and watch him till he gets used to his new home.''

"The more help I have the first half-hour the quicker supper will be ready,'' announced Jacintha, and immediately Georgie, Phillipa, Geraldine and Roberta shouted, "I'll help!'' not because they had much interest in cooking, but because they hoped to find out more about Jacintha and her mysterious "Dick.''

"Very well . . . here are four, strong, young scullions for you, Jacintha. Now we must all get to work. Miss Carroll, will you and Cecilia help Doris cut bread and butter while Miss Lyle and I look out the blankets. We shall need as many arms as we can get to spread them in the sun for an airing.''

"What are you going to cook for supper, Jacintha?'' asked Georgie.

"How can I tell until I see what is in the larder—

and oh, I say, please don't call me that—I'm always Jack, or Jacky."

"But why?"

"For the same reason you are called Georgie, I suppose. It suits me because I'm a sort of Jack of all trades and have had to turn my hand to anything. I'm doing it this moment."

"Don't you like cooking then?" demanded Geraldine.

Jacintha shrugged her shoulders. "I don't mind it . . . especially when it is difficult as it is now . . . it's a work of art then. Let's have a look at the fodder."

They went to the hut door through which Doris had vanished into a tiny kitchen. Two large oil-stoves stood together and the room contained little else except two high stools, a table, a vegetable rack, a sink and shelves holding rows of bright yellow crocks and dishes filled with provisions, pots and pans, spice and sugar boxes.

"Where is the meat?" asked the head cook.

"In the safe . . . you're never going to eat it raw. miss?" Doris looked scared and the four assistant cooks shrieked. A window in the north wall of the hut looked into the pine-wood and also into a big, hanging meat-safe where reposed the joints of meat which, according to Doris, were asking so pathetically to be cooked.

"It's mutton," announced Jacintha professionally. "What do you say to Lob's Scouse?"

"What on earth is that?"

"It's a nice dish for a camp feast because Lob is a sort of woodland creature though why a stew should

be named after him, goodness knows . . . but the
great thing is we've got all the things for making it."

"Then let's have it. What is it going to be cooked
in? A gipsy pot over the fire?"

"No, we haven't got a hanging pot and it would
be too slow anyway. We'll pop this in water to soak
while we make our kitchen."

Jacintha dropped the joints into a crock of spring
water and then led her helpers down to the beach
greatly to the vexation of the girls who were lugging
blankets into the sun, for they thought it pretty cool
to undertake the cooking and then rush off in a sort
of beach-combing expedition.

"We want lots of stones," was Jacintha's first order
and she began to fill the sack she had brought with
the largest stones she could find helped by the mysti-
fied scullions.

Three times a full sack was conveyed to a little
clearing in the pine-wood which Jacintha had decreed
should be her kitchen. There, with the stones, Jacintha
built up a chimney and instructed the others to build
another exactly like it. The tops of three chimneys and
one side, facing the wind, were left open and when
they were finished the crevices between the stones were
filled tightly with earth and dried grass.

Then they collected sticks and pine-cones and made
a roaring fire in each chimney which two of the girls
kept burning. The others went back to the kitchen
and fetched two large pans which Jacintha half-filled
with water and placed on the top of the chimneys.

"And now for the scouse," she said and asked
three of the girls to peel potatoes and onions while she
and Georgie cut up the meat.

Georgie volunteered to help with this distasteful task because she wanted Jacintha to think her a sport.

"We'll have the potatoes sliced. Lob likes them that way," said Jacintha. "But don't cut up the onions or you'll let out all the flavour."

When the ingredients were ready the cook put layers of potatoes, meat and onions in the pans until they were full when she put on the lids tightly.

"What about salt?" asked Roberta.

"We don't add that till it's nearly done . . . salt makes meat hard. I say, do go on stoking all of you, please, these pans must boil."

"Well, I'm not surprised cooks are hard to get," remarked Geraldine, who was one of the onion peelers and was still weeping copiously. "If they have to cry quarts every time there are onions for dinner it must be rather depressing."

"What is the next job?" asked Georgie.

"Get the pots to boil . . . we *must* stoke." And for the next ten minutes they poked wood into the chimneys until the pans began to boil over and immediately this happened Jacintha threw dried grass and earth on to the flames to reduce the heat remarking "that a stew boiled was a stew spoiled. Lob must now only gently simmer. In fact he'll look after himself for the next three hours except for an occasional shake . . . so we might as well go on with the breakfast."

"Breakfast! But we haven't had tea or supper yet!"

"I know . . . but that's a cook's life. She always has to think of the next meal before the last is eaten. But I can carry on myself now if you are all fed-up, you know."

To tell the truth the scullions were now very anxious to see what was going on in other directions and they were rather glad to see Ethel approaching with the confidence of one who has a message to deliver.

"Here's Ethel. I suppose she's coming to say that tea is ready."

"Well, I don't allow people in my kitchen," said Jacintha, who did not find Ethel attractive. "And I'm not a lady cook so I don't have tea with the family. I'll be obliged if you'll tell her so before she pokes her nose in here."

"But don't you want any tea?"

"I'm not very keen . . . anyway, I'm too busy," said Jacintha finally.

"You are all to come to tea," shouted Ethel. "And what on earth are those chimney arrangements?"

"Never you mind, and the new cook doesn't allow people poking round her kitchen," said Georgie. "Come along, girls," and then turning to Jacintha she gave her a friendly smile and whispered, "I'll bring you some fodder, cook," and then she hurried after the others to get rid of the disappointed and indignant Ethel.

Jacintha was left alone squatting near her fires and looking remarkably like an Indian squaw brooding over her cooking-pots.

CHAPTER IV

ROUND THE CAMP FIRE

As soon as Jacintha was left alone her expression changed from hard, independent defiance to wistful despair. Many a time during her wanderings with her bohemian step-father she had felt lonely, but never before had she felt unwanted. With her head resting on her bare, scratched knees she sat wondering if it would be better if she waited until darkness fell and then disappeared again to face an uncongenial life at the Vicarage. Anything would be better surely than thrusting herself upon people whom she felt despised her shabbiness.

Most schoolgirls wish for freedom and adventure, and often grumble at the dullness of home life; but Jacintha, in spite of her don't-care-what-I-do sort of attitude towards strangers was, in reality, a girl who longed to escape from free, roving ways and to have a conventional home and "belong" to someone who cared for her.

She sat up suddenly and muttered, "Well, I've done it now and they might not think I'm good enough for their blessed school; but anyway, I'll jolly well show them I can earn my keep," and jumping up she fed the fires and then, darting back to the kitchen returned with another huge cooking-pot, a bag of oatmeal and a pail of spring water. She measured the oatmeal into the pot with salt and water, stirred it well and set it aside. Then she scooped a hole in the ground and lined it thickly and tightly with dry grass. She was busy with this when footsteps approached.

"Bother! I wish they would leave me alone and let me just *be* the cook! I won't be patronised by a lot of schoolgirls."

It was Georgie—the girl she liked best—carrying a large cup of tea, a plate of bread and butter and a delicious, sugary bun.

"I've brought your tea."

"Thanks awfully." Having not the least idea that Georgie found her very interesting, Jacintha hoped devoutly that this girl would go away again and leave her to her meditations. But Georgie sat down and surveyed the hole.

"What's that for?"

"It's a sort of oven. When Lob is cooked I shall bring that pan of oatmeal to the boil on one of the chimneys, and then pop it into the hole and cover it tightly with grass and earth. It will be ready to serve as hot porridge in the morning."

"But how frightfully brainy of you to think of that."

"I didn't think of it. It's an old trick and when you haven't got any fuel you must cook with your wits."

"I'm awfully glad you are coming to our school."

"I don't know yet whether I *am* coming . . . the authorities haven't passed me." Jacintha gave her "don't care" grin. "And if I do stay I've decided to stay as camp cook."

"They want you in the school. I heard Sunny Jim say to Miss Lyle that you were 'a girl of resource,' the

sort of pupil the school needs. He's persuaded Bee—
we call Mrs. Bly that because she's so busy and sweet—
to write to that vicar at once and when she's got his
address Cecilia's going to ride to the post with the
letter."

"Which is Cecilia?"

"The tall, fair girl. She's sixteen and quite nice but
rather colourless. She writes poetry, but I couldn't
imagine her cooking porridge with her wits."

Jacintha began to cheer up for Georgie showed so
plainly that she thought it cleverer to be able to cook
than write poetry. "Aren't you going back?"

"Not unless you hate me being here. Bee said I
could stop and help you."

"There's nothing to do now, really, but, of course
I don't don't mind you staying." Jacintha drank her
tea and ate the food with appetite and feeling all the
better for it she got up to stoke the fires again just as
Mrs. Bly appeared.

"Well, Jacintha . . . you seem very busy and what
a delicious smell! It makes me quite hungry! Georgie
dear, go and help Sally and Anne carry in the
blankets."

Georgie went with reluctance and Mrs. Bly sat down
on the pine-needles.

"I'm writing to your friend, the Vicar, Jacintha,
when you have given me his name and address. I
shall tell him you are here and I think it would be a
good idea for him to tell your step-father you are joining us for a week or two, just to see how we like each
other, you know." She smiled, but Jacintha's face
went hard again.

"If I stay, I'd rather be the cook, please."

"But my dear child, what about your education?"

"I wasn't having any with Dick. He taught me heaps, of course, but nothing out of books."

"Have you any other accomplishments besides cooking, Jacintha?"

"I can speak French—Canadian French—I can ride anything and I can play the banjo."

"But you must understand that though we are camping at present this is a real school and though the girls mostly govern themselves and have few restrictions we expect good results as far as work is concerned from our pupils."

"Yes . . . that's why I'd rather be the cook . . . thanks awfully, all the same."

Feeling that this was a little too much for her after a strenuous day, Mrs. Bly smiled sweetly, "Well, we'll talk it over again, Jacintha. Write me the address on this envelope and then, if you can leave these pots and pans run away and ask Miss Lyle to show you your sleeping-quarters."

"Everything will be all right for an hour."

"Run along then."

When Jacintha came out of the pine-wood she saw a gay sight. The bright colours of the girls' frocks looked like flowers on the green, turfy downs and watching them flit about she was again overcome with deep depression. However hard she tried to carry off the situation nothing could alter the fact that *her* frock was a disgrace and those she had stuffed into her suit-case nearly as bad. The travelling bags and cases piled outside the huts were, she felt sure, filled with garments proper to all occasions and she supposed their owners regarded them entirely as a matter of course never having known a clothes shortage. For the hundredth time during the last two hours she wished Dick could have been a real father and could have come and faced these people himself and explained their unfortunate position.

Everyone seemed extremely busy. Doris was clearing the long tea-table set on the veranda of the largest hut. The Professor, Audrey and Cecilia were putting up tents; Miss Lyle was in one of the dormitory-huts shouting out directions from an open window to girls, who with shrieks of laughter, were carrying in blankets that had been sunning in the gorse-bushes. Christopher Columbus was rabbiting madly, while Felicity, sat on the caravan steps nursing her cat who was the only one except Jacintha who seemed not to be enjoying himself.

When she saw Jacintha approach Felicity called. " Jacintha, Father's made a run for your hens and what *do* you think? One of the darlings has laid an *egg*!"

"And do you think that's wonderful?"

"Of course. You would think they would be too homesick to think of such a thing yet . . . it's a lovely, long, white egg."

"Then you can have it for breakfast."

"Oh, Jachintha . . . can I really. Father, do you hear . . . the long, white egg is for *me*!"

"Don't go on harping on eggs, child. Jacintha, do you understand tent-raising? I've got as much as I can do in fixing up mine and I imagine those two girls next-door could do with a few hints."

"I know more about tents than I know about houses."

"No, Jim. You must not keep Jacintha now. She's been working hard ever since she arrived and now she wants to unpack. Go into that hut, child, and Miss Lyle will help you."

"And we don't need help, thank you, Professor—we've got a book of directions." Audrey's flushed face appeared at the tent door and regarded Jacintha a little haughtily.

Unaware that this was simply sixth form superiority Jacintha was furious and said as she passed, "You are pulling your guy-ropes—there'll be a heavy dew to-night and if they are as taut as that the ropes will contract when they get damp and pull out your pegs."

"Well, I must say!" gasped Audrey. "Is there *anything* that child doesn't know? What do we do, Cecilia? Ignore her advice, or loosen the ropes?"

"What does the book say?"

"Nothing. Did you ever know a text-book tell you the important thing?"

"Then let's loosen the ropes and if it's wrong we'll teach her not to give any more wrong information. Pass the hammer."

Jacintha took her suit-case from the donkey-cart and mounted the steps to the dormitory hut. Its spaciousness surprised her and her sense of neatness, acquired after much camping, delighted in the orderly rows of bunks one above another all covered with bright, yellow, coverlets.

There were sleeping quarters for twelve people and beneath the windows looking towards the sea were stools and tables for reading and writing. At each end of the hut was a smaller room, one fitted up for washing purposes and the other a sort of wardrobe room with rows of pegs and lockers. When Jacintha entered Miss Lyle was delivering a short lecture.

"Remember, *nothing* to be left about—this isn't a gipsy encampment. All clothes to be kept in lockers and coats and dressing-gowns hung on pegs. Every girl makes her own bed and on *no account* must she sit on it during the day. Oh, here you are Jacintha . . . that's your bed at the end. I'll give you a locker to-morrow when we are more settled."

"You mean you'll give me a locker when the Vicar has given me a character," thought Jacintha, and for a moment she rather wished he wouldn't.

"I hope you wear pyjamas—it's the rule here."

"Yes, I do." Jacintha flung down her suit-case trying to look unconcerned though in reality she shrank from the moment to come when she must don an old pair of Dick's pyjamas for out of the corner of her eye she could see on every bunk neatly folded garments in green, blue and mauve.

"Would you like me to unpack your night things?"

"Thanks awfully, but it won't take me a jiffy and I must be off now and give Lob a shake." Jacintha escaped from the curious eyes surrounding her and made her way to her woodland kitchen.

As she passed the central hut she could see through the open windows a long room with shelves round it where three of the older girls were arranging books, paint-boxes, cameras, games and puzzles. A long table ran down the centre. The kitchen and the store rooms were at the end of this hut and Doris could be heard singing as she washed up the tea things.

The third hut contained sleeping quarters for the staff.

When Jacintha reached her camp fires she felt more cheerful. Lob was simmering beautifully and a delicious fragrance was issuing from the cooking pots. She was stoking the fires when Georgie appeared again.

" Jacky—I'm not going to call you Jacintha—you are going to sleep in the bunk under me. I asked Miss Lyle to put you there . . . isn't it jolly?"

"Very," answered Jacky dryly, wondering what her new friend would think of a person who wore pyjamas several sizes too large for her with an odd patch on the jacket.

" I really wasn't going to sleep in a dormitory at all. The ' Blues ' and the ' Mauves ' are allowed to go under canvas, and I've got a stunning new tent —Christmas and birthday present combined—but the wretched people haven't sent it. It will be here to-morrow . . . at least I hope it will."

" You are lucky to have a tent. If you are going to camp it's better to be under canvas. I say, why do you all wear different colours?"

"Oh, some idea of Bee's. She thinks different colours belong to different ages and we ' respond ' to their influence. I think it is potty, myself."

" So do I. I never feel any different in a blue frock than I do in a pink, but perhaps that's because they are all washed out."

Georgie looked embarrassed and then said in a sort of burst as if she had that moment made up her mind, " Look here, Jacky, my tent really is for four people, but I don't mean to invite four people to share it because Jerry and I—you know Geraldine, she's frightfully nice and my chum—think it would be jollier to just

share it together; but if *you* will join us we'd like it
most awfully."

Jacky was astonished at such friendliness and
touched, too, but she said hastily, "It's jolly nice of
you to ask me but don't forget two's company and
three's none."

"Rubbish! We'll have lots of fun. Don't you think
it is rather queer we should all have boys' names—
Jacky, Jerry and Georgie?"

"Didn't I hear some girls called Joanna, Phillipa
and Roberta, too? If so, I suppose *they* could be Jo,
Phil and Bobby . . . we had better form a Boys'
Brigade."

Georgie's eyes sparkled. This sounded the sort of
thing one read about in school stories and she said,
"Oh, Jacky, *could* we? Wouldn't it be gorgeous?
I'd love to have a sort of club and so would Jerry
and to tell the truth I think we are going to be too
much under Bee's eye in spite of all this talk of freedom
and it would be perfect if we could organise something
entirely for ourselves."

Georgie looked at Jacky with such respect that at
last the new girl realised with something of a shock that
this new friend admired her and looked to her for
interesting ideas and amusement.

This was awkward because Jacky was in no mood
for schoolgirl mysteries, but it was pleasant to be
admired, and Jacky, almost happy, gave Lob a good
shake and said, "Well, we must think about it.
I say, this stuff will be ready in quarter of an hour—
do you mind spreading the good news?"

Georgie disappeared and Jacky lifted the lids of

the pots, stirred the contents, added salt and pepper and then went off to the kitchen.

"Doris?"

"Yes—miss." Doris was not quite sure of this particular young lady's status. Her faded frock and her knowledge of cooking puzzled her.

"We can't possibly provide hot plates, worse luck— so the next best thing is to serve the supper piping hot straight from the pot. Is everything ready?"

"Yes, miss." Doris looked with pride at the long table on the veranda set with a green check cloth and primrose coloured pottery.

"Well, ring the bell in five minutes, please, and when everyone is seated come and help me carry in the pans."

Jacky disappeared again happily concious that by arranging that she should help Doris serve she would again escape joining the party.

Everyone speedily obeyed the call to supper and when Mrs. Bly found that the serving was to be taken out of her hands she began to regard Jacintha Drew as a person worthy of respect.

Doris went down one side of the table with a steaming pot while Jacky served the other and in a few minutes everyone had before them a plate piled with hot, delicious stew.

Nothing could induce the cook to sit down, too. She said she must see to the breakfast and returned to her camp fires leaving Doris to serve the second helpings so much in demand.

Jacky stoked the fire in one of her chimneys again and then putting on the porridge-pot she stirred it until it came to the boil and then popped it quickly into the grass-lined hole and covered it thickly with grass and earth.

She was busy with this when the Professor and his wife appeared. "We've come to say thank you, Jacintha."

"I hope Lob was nice."

"Excellent! Excellent! Best meal I've tasted for ages, a homely dish with plenty of flavour and no frills." The Professor shook hands with her so solemnly that Jacky felt as if she had just passed some stiff examination with high honours.

"It was *very* good, Jacintha, and just the sort of meal we all needed. And now, my dear, I want you to have your supper at once . . . you must not hold yourself aloof in this way."

"But cooks always have their meals last."

"Not a temporary lady cook. Come along . . . Doris is enjoying hers and I want to see you sitting down, too."

The homeless "unwanted" feeling that had made Jacky so unhappy disappeared as attentions were showered upon her. A chair was drawn out for her and Cecilia stood behind it ready to serve the stew. The Professor poured out a glass of water and Felicity unrolled her table-napkin.

When supper was eaten the girls and the Professor went outside to sit on stools to watch the sunset and the Professor said to Jacky, "I suppose as you've been out west you know all there is to know about tents, young lady, now have you any criticism to make about my little rig-out?"

He pointed to a new white bell-tent proudly.

"It's a jolly tent—but if it had been mine I'd have

shoved it into a pail of green or brown dye before I put it up. That white is too dazzling for this open ground and you'll be worried by the light in the mornings."

"H'm . . . anything else?"

"You've put the door looking west. That's a mistake, I think, because the west wind prevails here . . . I should have turned my back to it."

"That's sound criticism, and I'm obliged. What sort of tenting had you in the wilds?"

"Oh, every kind. Dick knows every tent in the world, I should think. He's lived with eskimos in tents made of seal-skin and in an Arab's tent of woven hair. Once we both camped at the foot of the Rockies in a wigwam we bought from an Indian—it had the jolliest pictures all over it."

"Oh, Jacintha . . . have you really lived in a Red Indians' tent?" Felicity regarded her rapturously and Georgie demanded, "What sort of pictures?"

"Wait a moment, Georgie, my dear," interrupted the Professor. "I'm going to smoke my pipe of peace and while I do it it would be an excellent idea if you all made a camp fire. I think we ought to have one to-night to celebrate our arrival—perhaps Jacintha will direct, but don't make it *too* close to the tents."

"Are they idiots, or is he just treating them like idiots?" thought Jacky amazed at such a warning. As nobody else began to work she found a sandy patch on the turf and scooped out a ditch in the shape of a cross and put pebbles at the bottom of it. She then asked everyone to collect cones and wood and soon there was a fire leaping upwards and the girls surrounded it in a circle with the Professor now ready to make a speech.

"Just now, girls, Jacintha touched on a very interesting subject, Red Indian wigwams and last term we all read 'Hiawatha' and learnt how the Indian believes in the 'Great Spirit' and how nature provides him with his gods. You will—I hope—remember the description of Hiawatha's wigwam:

Made of deerskins dressed and whitened,
With the gods of the Dacotahs
Drawn and painted upon the curtains.

Jacintha, has not only provided us with a well cooked camp meal, but she has suggested a subject for our first powwow round the camp fire. I'm going to ask her to explain those pictures on the Red Indian tent she once actually lived in, pictures which of course had something to do with the Red Indian family who made it . . . Jacintha, my dear, we are waiting."

For a moment Jacky was completely aghast at finding herself, after all her efforts to remain unseen as the camp cook, suddenly called upon to address the pupils of Rainbow End on Indian folklore. In the presence of a learned Professor, too! Her embarrassment was increased by hearing a titter from Ethel Forbes.

Then looking at the Professor's kind eyes beaming at her through his spectacles she realised he understood that she was sensitive about her short-comings and was expressing his sympathy by giving her a chance to show she knew something on other subjects besides cooking.

Determined to be greatful for this, she glared at Ethel, swallowed the lump in her throat and began to speak:

"I suppose you all know that a wigwam is conical in shape and made of deerskins or buffalo skins sewn together?"

The older girls looked wise, but Felicity said frankly, "No, we don't."

"First of all three straight poles are tied together at the top and then spread out at the base like a tripod. Then ten more poles are placed round at equal distances, their tops falling into the forks made by the first three, like this." Jacky made a little model of sticks. "The skins are then drawn over the frame and the edges pinned together over the door opening. The wigwam is pegged tightly down all round to keep out draughts and two ear-poles regulate the draught of the smoke-hole in the top. It's awfully snug inside with a circle of stones in the middle for the cooking-fire and round this the beds are made of skins. The Indians have jolly times round the fire, dancing and telling stories."

"But what about the pictures on your tent?"

"At the very top there was painted a broad band of black—that meant night. On this black band there was a gold Evening Star and a large butterfly which means 'Sleep-Bringer.' I think the family must have been under the protection of the fire-fly because after the black band came a jolly procession of fireflies all round the tent. Then came a brown band, and this meant the earth and the little points all along it meant the Rocky Mountains."

"What did you do with your wigwam?"

"Dick sold it. We couldn't trail round with it, worse luck."

"Oh dear," sighed Georgie, "why didn't I know

all this before and choose a wigwam instead of the latest up-to-date guide's tent?"

"I can see Miss Carroll waving from the veranda, which means she wants you, Felicity, my child, and in a few minutes Miss Lyle will blow a whistle which she has most unfortunately acquired to call you all in," said the Professor. "We have only a few minutes left to enjoy the best part of camp life so I'll just propose a vote of thanks to Jacintha for her interesting lecture on the Indian wigwam and then set your work for to-morrow."

"Oh, Professor . . . do we have to begin work at once?"

"Yes, to-morrow . . . every man jack of you, big and little. You are all requested to make a model wigwam with a design suitable to this camp's family history. The design I like best I shall adopt for my own tent as I've always wanted to be a Red Indian Chief. The winner of the design shall have a reward . . . she shall help me paint the design on my wigwam. There; the whistle—good night!"

CHAPTER V

THE BOYS' BRIGADE

VERY early one morning exactly three weeks after Jacintha Drew's extraordinary appearance at Rainbow End an old woman came panting up the steps that led from the shore to the camping-ground and gazed around her with delighted astonishment.

The windows of the huts were all wide-open but there

was not a sign of life to be seen. The open caravan, too, was silent, though a tabby cat sat on the top step yawning.

Five tents with their flaps pinned back were pegged out in a semi-circle on the green turf and the decorations on two of them made the old woman stare and chuckle loudly.

The largest tent—the Professor's—was no longer dazzlingly white for a gaily-painted design was splashed all over it. This was the winning design sent in by Jacintha Drew.

Round the top was a deep band of black, representing the night sky without a single star, the Professor being known to prefer dark nights for his moth-hunting. Below the blackness of night blazed the "Golden Eye of Heaven," the bright orb of the Sun. This meant that the chief was a sun-worshipper and desired his pupils to get all the sun rays they could for their health's sake. Next, came a procession of brown owls, a pretty compliment to the Chief's well-known wisdom, and below these came the rolling downs in bright green filled with the choicest botanical specimens in all colours. Over the arch of the door was the best inspiration of all, a gorgeous, many-coloured rainbow its end resting in painted crocks of gold. At the very top of the tent blazed a magnificent top-knot of sea gulls' feathers dyed scarlet, a reminder that this was the wigwam of the Chief.

Three of the tents were plain without decoration, but the fifth, a green canvas, made the old woman chortle again.

It was Georgie Kent's "stunner" though the firm that made it would never have known it now decorated to Georgie's ideas of Red Indian principles. There was again the black band of night, but it was lavishly sprinkled with all the stars of the firmament. Having been told by Jacky that when building his home the Indian takes the first thing he sees on waking for his totem or mascot, Georgie went to bed in high excitement and on waking opened her eyes on the wide, blue sea. She decided she was to be specially watched over by Neptune and his creatures and because dolphins are decorative and easy to draw she painted a row of them swimming gaily round the tent in a sea of deep blue with a broad border of cockle-shells.

As the old woman stood staring at this a girl ran out of the dolphin tent towards her. She had short, reddish hair, a thin, brown face, rather anxious looking, and she wore a frock of blue belted with white—Jacintha Drew transformed into a Rainbow End schoolgirl! Exciting things had happened to her since she joined the camp, the most exciting being a letter from her step-father containing five pounds "to buy some togs and things." Like a sensible girl Jacky had gone to Mrs. Bly for advice about the spending of what seemed to her a vast sum and that lady, very tactfully said she would send for the things Jacky needed from town. She secretly added what more was necessary and Jacky became the owner of a modest outfit and a respectable "Blue." The Vicar had written, too, and though it was plain that he was surprised that his invitation had been scorned he spoke well of Jacky and her step-father adding that they were "extremely unconventional" and implied that he really meant they were both a little mad.

Finding **cooks** were non-existent in the neighbour-

hood and afraid to import another town specimen the
Rainbow Camp school would have been in a nice fix
if Jacky had not turned out competent to cook meals
for them all; sometimes in her field-kitchen, and sometimes on the oil-stoves. After she had done this for
nearly three weeks the Professor came and thanked
her solemnly and told her that they not only owed her
eternal gratitude but a term's school fees. Happily
aware that she had "earned her keep," Jacky began
to look less tragic and defiant and consented to allow
her Japanese prints to be carefully packed away. Mrs.
Bly insisted on paying for all eggs laid by the
hens and Slowboy, the donkey became very useful as
an errand-boy for the whole camp.

"Good morning . . . are you Mrs. Jeans, the new
cook?"

"Ay . . . I be Kate Jeans, and who may you be,
missy?"

"I'm Jacintha Drew, the old cook, and I'm frightfully glad to see you because to tell the truth I'm sick
of it. I thought I had better turn out early and show
you how to manage things."

"Bless you dearie. I've cooked for a hotel before
I married Sam."

"How jolly. I'll take you to see the stoves first . . .
we cook with oil mostly."

"I cooked with oil before you was born, miss . . .
and I've cooked in ranges, and with them gas-stoves
and all . . . be the missus up?"

"Oh, no. You see she's got too much to do to be
bothered with cooking and housekeeping . . . *you'll*
have to do all that. I do think it's good of you to come,
Mrs. Jeans, do you have to walk far?"

"Do 'ee know that bit of a cottage up Sandy Lane?"

"That jolly little black house near the shore with the old wooden figurehead over the door?"

"That's right, miss. Me and my Sam have lived there over thirty year."

"And is your husband the fisherman with the boat called the *Seabird*?"

"That's my Sam. He don't do much fishing nowadays and I'd have been glad to oblige you before this if I'd known—fishing and beachcombing don't bring in what they did."

"Oh, Mrs. Jeans . . . do you go beachcombing?"

"Ay, us goes . . . Sam and me does, and we've found a thing or two in our time: but now it's mostly old fountain pens and them sixpenny brooches we picks up. Sam did find a set of false teeth a week or two back, but what's the good 'o they when they won't fit we? Where's the kitchen, miss?"

"Here it is." Jacky led the new cook into the tiny kitchen with its big stoves and spotless pots and pans.

"Bacon and eggs, I suppose, miss?"

"Oh, no . . . just porridge, brown bread and butter, marmalade, honey and fruit."

"Well, I'll do me best, I'm sure, miss, but it do seem queer to see gentlefolk living like a lot of gipsies and I laughed till I cried when I seen them painted tents."

"Oh, Mrs. Jeans, you *mustn't* call us gipsies! We are the tidiest people and most well behaved and clean. I'm just going to have my bathe now. Goodbye, it *is* jolly having you."

"Well I never," muttered Mrs. Jeans tying on an

apron as Jacky seized a bell from the veranda and rang it loudly before she disappeared.

In the tent she found Georgie and Jerry rolled in blankets on low camp-beds.

"Where *have* you been?"

"And *why* on earth are you dressed?"

"Well, I thought it wouldn't look well to interview the new cook in my bathing-togs and I told Bee I would show her round. She's a real old dear named Kate Jeans and she lives in that black cottage and she and Sam Jeans go beachcombing."

"What fun . . . can we go? I'd love to find coins from chests lost in the Spanish Armada and things like that."

"They've all been picked up years ago. Mrs. Jeans says they find nothing now but sixpenny brooches from Woolworths and false teeth they can't wear!"

The girls lay shrieking with laughter at the Jeans' beachcombing finds while Jacky undressed and pulled on her bathing suit.

"Aren't you two going to turn out?"

"I think I'll cut the early bathe and have what Doris calls a 'dip' with the delicate dears." Jerry snuggled down in her blanket.

Jacky surveyed her coldly and looked at Georgie.

"Are *you* coming?"

"I suppose so . . . I do wish, Jacky, that you would realise that these Spartan ways are *not* compulsory. We might as well be at a proper school where everyone has to obey rules by the way you go on."

"It's a pity you are not if you can't do the proper thing without anyone shoving you."

Georgie got out of her blankets and the two girls,

clad in green bathing-suits joined the other bathers including the Professor and Doris, who was no longer a pale-faced little Cockney.

Christopher Columbus, the terrier, led the way down the wooden steps to the shore and Cato, the cat, strolled to the top of the cliff and stared at the proceedings with the contempt all cats show for any actions they do not practise themselves.

Ten minutes were given to rythmic movements on the beach under the guidance of Miss Carroll in which the Professor joined with such comical solemnity it was as much as his pupils could do to restrain their mirth. Then came ten minutes in the sea until Miss Carroll blew a whistle and everyone scampered up the steps again to dress.

Breakfast was served on the long veranda and Ethel Forbes, who could not forgive Jacky for always politely ignoring her, said, " How delicious the porridge is this morning."

"Yes . . . *almost* as nice as Jacky's," answered Georgie loyally and glaring at Ethel.

"How very lucky we are to get Mrs. Jeans," added Mrs. Bly amiably, "for now Jacintha can join in all our lessons. What do you propose to do this morning, child? Miss Lyle will give mathematics for an hour. I am taking the 'Mauves' sketching, and the Professor is going to talk on the Romans in Dorset and anyone interested may walk with him over to the old earth works."

It seemed strange to hear a head-mistress asking her pupils how they intended to fill in their morning-hours but that was Mrs. Bly's way. Her theory was that if one felt in the mood for a certain subject that was the proper time to study it. New pupils learning this thought they had entered a scholastic paradise, but they soon discovered there was what they called "a snag," in the working of this method. You *could* dodge French, mathematics and other subjects, but if you continued to dodge them and failed at the end of the month's "trials" as they were called, a sort of cold disgrace fell upon the culprit.

At Mrs. Bly's question all Jacky's admirers looked at her fervently, trying to mesmerise her into saying she would join the Professor's expedition; but, to their surprise, she said calmly, "I think I'll have a go at the maths, please . . . I don't know a thing about them."

Miss Lyle beamed and Felicity said, "Oh Jacky, I *do* hope you are worse than I am."

It was nice after breakfast not to have to think about the cooking, but to fly about in the sun with Georgie and Jerry spreading out their bedding and making their tent ship-shape.

Georgie said, "Now you have finished with the cooking, Jacky, and no longer have to swot in the kitchen . . . what about the Boys' Brigade? You said you would think about it, didn't she, Jerry?"

"So you told me."

Jacky gave an inward sigh. She was afraid of this and had joined the maths class on purpose to avoid walking with her friends. She was grateful to Georgie for her friendship at a time when she was lonely and unappreciated and wished to show her gratitude; but she had no wish to be what she called "silly and school-girlish," and organise any sort of secret society. She felt, too, that Mrs. Bly would not like it and it would be disloyal after so much kindness.

"Did I?" she said carelessly. "Well I suppose I must then. I'll think about it and draw up some rules."

"Oh good! Shall we ask the other 'boys' to join? Phillipa is jolly and so is Roberta; but Joanna is a bit superior."

"All the better . . . we don't want to have all birds of one feather exactly. Let us be thankful though that Ethel was not christened anything boyish."

"Here's Joanna now,"

Joanna Treherne wore glasses and had a passion for reading. She did not in the least look like a candidate for a Boys' Brigade.

"Girls. Miss Carroll told me to tell you that there's to be a second bathe at twelve."

She walked off after casting a rather superior smile round their wigwam.

"A second bathe! How jolly!" Two of the girls rejoiced, but Jacky said, "I shan't bathe again—if there's time to spare I want to write to Dick."

"And don't forget those rules, my good lad," cried Georgie. "It's jolly at Rainbow and I'm enjoying it, but I am getting a bit sick of all this folk-dancing. Come along, Jerry, there is the Professor."

Jacky joined Miss Lyle's arithmetic class and for the first time in her life discovered what a difference an excellent teacher could make to the difficulties of learning and thoroughly enjoyed her first morning at school.

At eleven-thirty she was free and sat under a gorse-bush to write a letter to her step-father.

Dearest Dick,

I hope you had my letter before you sailed and

will find the others waiting for you when you arrive. It was *jolly* of you to send me such a fortune, but I am horribly worried about it really as I'm sure it means you have to starve or travel steerage! I love Rainbow End—no end—as a place. But I still feel an outsider and have to struggle to keep my end up. The Professor is a darling—I like him better than anyone here and he's been a trump to me. He's living in a wigwam and calls himself the Chief and thoroughly enjoys being one. He is round and tubby and has to crawl in and out of the door in the most killing way, but he says "Great men never mind stooping" (Ruskin). Mrs. Bly is nice, too; she's full of new ideas and yet all the time she's really rather old-fashioned. The girls are all so-so nobody is very exciting, though I like Georgie Kent and her chum, Jerry. They are dying for me to get up a secret society, or club or something and seem to think I'm the one to lead it as they have an idea you are a sort of Roy Rogers or Dare Devil Dick and we both lived like pirates for years. It seems I promised to do this in a moment of madness so I'll have to get up something; but I'm afraid they will be disappointed when they see the Rules and I hope they'll back out. I don't want to be like a girl in one of those silly school-books—*The Leader of the Rebels*, or *The Worst Girl in the School*. We have at last got a new cook, so now I am a lady pupil and have already disgraced you in the arithmetic class. Oh Dick, I simply *howl* with home-sickness sometimes and miss you terribly. Please send for me the very minute you can afford it.

Much love, Jacky

P.S.—The hens, Billy Slowboy and the Japanese prints are all enjoying themselves.

When this epistle was finished Jacky sighed heavily, sucked her pencil, and then began to write again.

The Boys' Brigade

Rule I

The members of this society pledge themselves not to ape the manners and speech of boys unduly, but to adopt a manly and gentlemanly attitude towards life in general, never showing feminine weakness, or sentimentality in times of hardship or danger.

Rule II

Every member must acquire expert knowledge of at least one practical craft or art.

Rule III

The word "sweet" is taboo in speaking of clothes and behaviour.

Rule IV

The B.B. is not a secret society.
Everything concerning it is open and above board. It is not intended, however, that members should babble to outsiders of the B.B.'s doings, which will be mainly for the good of the community.

Unnecessary tongue-wagging is therefore sternly discouraged.

Rule V

The watchword of the B.B. is COMPETENCE.
The motto: "Facta non verba."

God Save The Queen!

"There! If they don't like it they can jolly well get one up themselves and leave me out of it. What on earth is the matter down there?"

Cries of consternation were ascending from the beach and Jacky, rushing to the steps, discovered the cause. Miss Carroll, white and shivering was standing in her bathing-suit dripping with water, and the twelve-o'clock bathers, all dripping salt water, too, were all talking at once while Miss Carroll counted them aloud like an anxious shepherd of sheep.

"*Two* of you are missing! Heavens! It's Felicity and Ethel! Yet I *know* they came out of the sea."

"They must have gone back into the sea again, Miss Carroll."

"But what *terrible* disobedience! Don't move, any of you . . . I must go back at once." More alarmed than she had ever been in her life at the total disappearance of two girls in her care, Miss Carroll began to race back to the sea thinking of all the bathing fatalities she had heard of in the past.

At that moment, Jacky, from her vantage post up above saw Ethel's head pop up out of a rocky pool and Felicity's from another.

"Miss Carroll! Miss Carroll!" she shouted. "They are over there . . . hiding in the rock pools!"

She flew down the steps and the culprits, highly indignant, crawled out of the pools.

Miss Carroll looked as if she might faint, some of the girls laughed, but Jacky was scathing.

"Felicity . . . how *could* you be such a little idiot . . . ? but I bet you didn't think of such a silly trick!"

"No, I didn't . . . but what's the matter with everyone? We were only pretending we were drowned."

"And, besides, it's nothing to do with you," cried Ethel.

Then Miss Carroll came to life and at the same moment Cecilia and Audrey trotted up on their ponies and demanded the reason for the commotion.

"Commotion! Let me tell you, Cecilia, it might have been something much worse than a commotion. These two little idiots actually hid from me in the rock pools and say they were *pretending to be drowned*."

"And Jacky spotted them," explained Sally Parker.

"I always said green bathing suits were a mistake," said Audrey. "They ought to be scarlet and then nobody could play tricks."

"Do you want us to deal with them, Miss Carroll?" asked Cecilia.

When Mrs. Bly had told Jacintha the girls pretty well governed themselves she meant that misdemeanour in work or behaviour was dealt with by Cecilia and Audrey who could appeal to a higher court if they found a problem too difficult.

"I'd hand them over to the Chief," advised Jacky. "And I hope he cuts their bathe for a week at least."

"And I would like to hand *you* over to him for interfering," shouted Ethel. "And I hope he puts you in your proper place." Ethel's tone inferred that Jacky's proper place was not at Rainbow End.

"Be quiet—all of you, and run *at once* to change. I shall see how this shall be dealt with later." Miss Carroll and her charges marched away to dress and Jacky was left with the older girls.

"What happened exactly, Jacky?"

"The little donkeys hid themselves . . . they must have held their breath under the water for they really couldn't be seen. Miss Carroll was in an awful stew. I'm not the head girl I know and never shall be, but after the talk I have heard about expressing one's individuality and thinking out things for ourselves I think I might dare to criticise a little."

"Do you mean you want to criticise *me*?" Cecilia looked amused.

"Not especially. I mean the system . . . there's too much rhythmic movement and Greek dancing in this school and not enough cricket, which I think would be better for the whole lot of us."

"Do you indeed? Well, suppose, now that you are a pupil in the school, you put your suggestion to the Committee which, as it happens, meets at five this afternoon."

"And do you—may we ask, play cricket yourself?" inquired Audrey.

"Yes I *do*." Jacky's eyes flashed. "Wherever Dick and I have ever been we have always managed to get a team together, and I'm jolly glad we did."

Jacky walked off and Cecilia shrugged her shoulders, "We are going to have a rebel in the fourth form,

Audrey. *You* know the sort of thing that one reads in school stories—grievances, strikes, and everyone displaying a *grande passion* for the rebel."

"We can soon squash that. All the same, I've sometimes wondered myself if all this posturing is good for us. We could get just as much benefit from an honest game of cricket and it wouldn't make us so self-conscious."

"But Bee loves to see us throwing ourselves in lovely attitudes . . . cricket wouldn't look half so picturesque, and you know how she loathes girls who play hockey."

"Well, anyway, that Drew girl is a character and now she has left off stirring the porridge I believe she intends to stir up all Bee's precious pies and put her fingers in them, too. Off you go!"

The two girls clapped their hands and sent their ponies scampering over the downs and then sat down on the beach to sun-bathe.

When Georgie and Jerry were dressed they sought out Jacky and found her cleaning out the hen-run.

"I say Jack . . . I'm glad you snubbed Ethel. Have you made the Rules?"

"Yes, here they are." Jacky gave them the paper and they both read it with a slight disappointment for they had hoped for more daring things from an adventurer like Jacky and *Rule IV* at once became unpopular.

"I think it ought to be secret."

"I don't."

"Very well . . . but what shall we do first?"

"Learn cricket . . . that is if you can't play."

"We've never learnt." Georgie's disappointment deepened. "It's not one of our school games, and isn't it rather slow?"

"It's not so exciting as football, of course . . . but as we can't play that I thought cricket——"

"Oh, all right. We'll tell the others."

"I mean we'll get the whole camp to play, according to *Rules*. Dick was in the First XI at Harrow, so I've had a jolly good coaching."

"How nice. Shall we fetch the rest of the boys?"

"Not till after lunch . . . there's the bell now. I wonder what Mrs. Jeans will give us."

Mrs. Jeans had provided a well-cooked meal and it was decided that she was one of the treasures found at Rainbow End.

After lunch Jacky slipped off to the kitchen to tell her so. "Mrs. Jeans, that apple-pudding was marvellous."

"Ay. I've got a light hand for puddins. It's pretty of you, missy, to come and tell me you enjoyed it . . . I like to see young folk with manners. Look-ee, I've got everything ready for supper and I must get off to my Sam, now."

"I wish I could come with you. I do love your cottage, Mrs. Jeans."

"Do 'ee? I tell you what, dear. You shall come and take a cup o' tea along me and Sam some day. How would 'ee like that, now?"

"I'd simply *love* it. Thank you awfully, Mrs. Jeans."

Jacky walked to the steps with the old woman happily, little dreaming that her visit to the queer little black house in the lane would be the beginning of a remarkable adventure.

CHAPTER VI

NEPTUNE'S COTTAGE

To the school's surprise Miss Carroll did haul off the culprits to the tent of the Chief, and what is more the Chieftainess, Mrs. Bly, and her right hand, Miss Lyle, were requested to be present and decide on suitable chastisement. This put the authorities in a dilemma for they detested punishment though they realised that something must be done to people who feigned death just for the fun of it. To make matters more difficult, Miss Carroll became suddenly orthodox and demanded that the offenders should not be merely reasoned with and admonished but have a real old-fashioned punishment. She suggested that they should not be allowed to bathe for a week—except in a hip-bath in the dormitory for which they carried the water themselves.

This distressed the Professor because Felicity, his one ewe lamb, adored the sea and the daily bathe was already doing miracles for the delicacy that was one of the reasons they had come to Rainbow End.

Mrs. Bly, too, disliked the idea and thought it wrong to inflict an injury in return for an injury inflicted by mischievousness rather than malice. Miss Lyle sided with Miss Carroll and said she did not believe in heart-to-heart talks with the young and personally she had been longing for quite a week to give Ethel Forbes a real old-fashioned smack.

Cecilia and Audrey, also summoned to the council were both on the side of punishment.

"The young are so hard on each other," Mrs. Bly thought regretfully and then she said brightly, "Well, Jim, dear, you are the Chief and whatever you decide about it we must obey," and smiling sweetly she said she must hurry away to her history class.

The amiable Professor then became so much distressed that Miss Lyle said with amusement, "How about scalping them, Chief? Here's Jacintha Drew coming along. I'm sure she will be able to tell you the best and most scientific way of doing it."

"And that reminds me," added Miss Carroll, "Ethel deserves further punishment for speaking to Jacintha most rudely about being ' put in her place '!"

"Dear me! That was most unkind." The Professor was upset to think his favourite's feelings had been hurt.

"Jacintha thinks we all ought to play cricket," put in Cecilia.

"Are we not rather wandering from the point?" rebuked Miss Carroll.

"Not according to Jacintha," answered Cecilia politely and the Professor's eyes began to gleam behind his spectacles for he thought he saw a means of escape.

"My dears," he said. "Would you mind if we decided to settle this annoying little affair later? I can see Jacintha wants to speak to me and I told her she must come to me in any difficulty."

Miss Carroll could hardly object and the company melted away and Jacintha, hovering outside, was told to come in.

"Well, my child . . . what can I do for you?"

"I just wanted to ask you if you were keen on cricket?"

"Bless you . . . I was once my school's champion bowler."

Jacky beamed. "I knew you must be, somehow . . nice people always *are* keen on cricket. I've just been to the village."

"With permission, I hope, my dear." The Professor tried to remember he was a schoolmaster.

"Of course . . . I had to go to complain about the butter. I had a chat with an old man outside the shop and he told me they've got a marvellous village cricket team . . . quite 'pro' in fact. There's going to be a match this evening at five and I thought if you were keen you might like to go."

"I should indeed . . . would you like to go, child?"

"Oh, Professor, I'd *love* it! Would Mrs. Bly let me?"

"Why not? Run in now and ask her, and tell her to expect us back when she sees us, and look here, my dear, you might say, too, that I would rather she dealt with those two naughty children, as I know she will do it better."

"Of course I will." Jacky flew away to deliver her message and also left a note of her own at Cecilia's tent saying she was sorry she could not attend the committee meeting, but she was going with the Professor to a cricket match.

"What next, I wonder?" Cecilia said when she had read it. "I must say though, the child's got some manners. She needn't have told me she was not going to turn up."

The cricket enthusiasts did not return till nine o'clock.

The younger girls had gone to bed, but the older ones

were sitting on the veranda steps having a sing-song.

Georgie and Jerry looked at Jacky with reproach for they thought she might have managed an invitation for them to go with the Professor, too.

The two truants were full of praise for the village cricket team. It seemed that Broomy Hill was famous for good cricket which was why the inn was called *The Bat and Ball*. Sixty years before the team had actually played against professionals and nearly won, and there was some talk of having a similar match that summer and the Professor was to give his patronage.

"And we are going to play cricket at Rainbow End, my dear," he announced to his wife who had joined them. "With this excellent green I can't think why I did not think of it before."

"But Jim, that's our dancing green."

"You don't want to dance all the time and cricket is good for the character. If Ethel and Felicity had been cricketers they would not have played that foolish trick this morning."

Cecilia and Audrey exchanged amused glances and Jacky looked innocent.

"But I'm not sure if I want them to rush about after cricket balls." Mrs. Bly thought folk-dancing much more graceful.

"Nonsense, Beatrice—it is what they need. What is it, my pet?"

Felicity, in a rose-coloured dressing-gown came from the caravan carring a large pail of water carefully.

"Look Papa . . . it's some sort of jelly fish. We found it when we were wading. What is its name and is its sting deadly?"

"It is the *Cyanea* child . . . a common specimen.

See, there is its mouth with frilled lips. Those long, streamers contain the stinging cells; but they are not deadly, only disagreeable."

"I rather thought I'd keep it as a pet," said Felicity, but the Professor objected to this on the grounds that nothing consisting of ninety per cent. water was really desirable for a pet.

"I'll chuck it back into the sea, poor beastie," said Jacky and she seized the pail and rushed to the shore and the others gave sighs of relief.

When Jacky returned and entered the tent she found Georgie and Jerry sitting on their beds brushing their hair and their manner seemed a little cold. Disappointed that Jacky did not seem to notice it, Georgie said reproachfully, "You *might* have asked Sunny Jim to take us, too."

"But I did not know you were keen on cricket. You seemed jolly indifferent about it, this morning. What's happened about Ethel and Felicity? I believe the dear old Chief went off to get out of the mess!"

"They have both apologised to Miss Carroll and they are to bathe *before* breakfast, or not at all for a week. That's a *real* punishment for Ethel and she is the real culprit—personally I can't abide her," said Jerry.

"We've asked Roberta, Phillipa, and Joanna to join the B.B.," announced Georgie.

"Well?" Jacky hoped they had all refused.

"Phillipa said she was not keen on societies. Joanna refused absolutely—not highbrow enough for her—but Roberta is game."

"And she wants to be called 'Bert.' She says it sounds more dashing than 'Bobby'."

"Well, that makes four of us, you can tell 'Bert' we don't want members to be dashing. I'll be Jack, I think, and you Georgie had better be George."

"And I suppose I must stick to Jerry," sighed Geraldine.

"Then that's settled. We'll call a meeting soon and decide something definite."

"What do you suppose we will do first?" enquired Georgie eagerly.

Jacky had not the least idea what the B.B. would do first, or last for the matter of that; but she felt sorry for Georgie and Jerry who had spent the evening folk-dancing while she had been enjoying cricket so she promised to think about it.

Just before she went to sleep she said, "Georgie, do you mind if I ask old Mrs. Jeans to look inside the wigwam to-morrow? She is frightfully tickled by the outside."

"Of course not. Let's ask her to tea."

"Thanks awfully . . . she'll love that."

Tent dwellers were allowed to show hospitality and Georgie was dying to use her new tea-service of shell pink suitably decorated with green seaweed in honour of her totem, Neptune.

At four o'clock the next day Mrs. Jeans was conducted to the wigwam by Jacky and found Georgie, Jerry and Roberta awaiting her. Roberta had dropped in to see what was going on and seeing tea in preparation and a plate of the best mixed biscuits set out she fished for an invitation and got it.

Mrs. Jeans was charmed with everything. The wooden beds, the straps and pockets ingeniously let into the walls of the tent for its owner's small possessions, the tiny windows covered with a flap and best of all the attentions she received from four nice young ladies. She was installed in a camp chair with a cushion at her back and her feet upon a grass mat. A stool was placed near her to hold her cup and plate and the tea was hot and strong and the mixed biscuits excitingly varied. The girls gave the old woman a good time and before she left they received an unexpected and delightful reward.

She invited them all to visit her at the Black Cottage the following day to "take a cup o' tea with me and Sam."

From the first moment they had seen this cottage when rambling along the shore every girl in the school had been fascinated by its queerness. The black tarred walls looked interestingly ancient, and the tiny garden which surrounded it might have been a mermaid's garden at the bottom of the sea. Instead of flowers it was filled with shells and corals picked up on the beaches of the world and all arranged in flower-like patterns. A path of flints led to the cottage door grey-gold in colour and shaped as round as moons by the endless crash and gnash and draw of tides when they lay upon the shore. Above the door hung the wooden figurehead of an old ship, *Neptune*, with gilt still on his trident and flakes of blue paint decorating his wooden mantle.

The cottage, too, had a most intriguing summer-house, an old boat cut in two standing up on its cut end, the curved bow forming a roof. The locker of the boat provided a seat for two and it smelt of lobster, seaweed and salt breezes.

The sandy shore heaped itself outside the cottage gate and flew into every crevice in the cottage during a storm, but in fine weather it seemed an ideal residence to the girls.

The four invited to visit it were madly envied; in fact Felicity almost shed tears at their departure.

They set out in high spirits, Georgie, especially, feeling uproariously happy because she felt the portents were good for this first excursion of the B.B. for here Neptune was the Jeans' totem too, and had probably arranged the whole affair.

Sam Jeans was sitting on his boat *Seabird*, smoking a pipe and meditating.

"There's Sam. I do wish he would invite us to go fishing with him."

"Perhaps he will."

"I'd rather he took us beachcombing."

"Look! There's a yacht or a smack or some sort of ship anchored out there. I wonder who owns it?"

"Let's ask Sam." Jacky took the lead and advancing boldly said, "Good afternoon, Mr. Jeans, we've come to have tea with you."

"That's right, you be all welcome, I'm sure."

"Is that ship out there what is called a fishing-smack?" asked Georgie.

"Nay, she be a yacht and she belongs to a London gent."

"What's her name?"

"*La Belle Dame*, he calls her, says it means 'Lovely Lady,' but my missus says don't you believe it."

The girls concealed their mirth and Jacky asked, "What is a cutter, Mr. Jeans?"

"Her would carry one mast, and a big mainsail,"

"And a yawl?" asked Jacky, determined to show she had some knowledge of seacraft.

"Her carries a little mast in her stern, missy, and a big mast forarder with a smaller mainsail."

"And a schooner?" asked Roberta.

"Two masts in her middle, and her's a fine, big boat."

"Thanks awfully, we want to find out all we can about ships," said Jacky, who had just decided that this knowledge would be good for the B.B., and enormously interesting to herself.

"Ay, ships take a lot o' beating," said Sam. "And they knows more—much more—than most folks guesses, there's bad and good among 'em just as among folks. You want to be aboard a ship in a gale to get to know her. There's the missus waiting above."

Mrs. Jeans, in a clean apron and a magenta beret perched coquettishly on her grey locks was standing at the cottage door holding a black cat in her arms, and they rushed to pay their respects.

"What a lovely cat! What's his name?"

"Poacher, miss. He be a rare one for bringing home rabbits and us gets many a nice stew, bless him. Come in and welcome."

The interior of Neptune's cottage was even more intriguing than the exterior and mysteriously dark because the window was little more than a spy-hole looking out to sea.

Fishing-tackle, sea-boots, oilskins, etc, were flung down in its dark corners and out of the farthest and most dim loomed a wooden figure of a mermaid gaily-painted and carring a lyre. She seemed to be the family hat-stand and garments of all kinds, including Mrs. Jeans' Sunday bonnet, were suspended from nails knocked into her wooden sides.

"Oh what is that?" Roberta was startled.

"That be t'old figurehead of the *Seamaid*, miss. Her were a fine ship a hundred years ago and Sam's grandfather captained her. Sit ye down and make yerselves at home."

A fire of driftwood leapt on the hearth and suspended over it was a black kettle. On the tall chimney-piece stood a row of shining pewter plates which gave a homely gleam to the dark room. A row of pot-dogs stood in front of them and on the wall above hung a stuffed shark.

A round table was laid for tea and the floral decorations were delightfully original. In the centre of the white cloth stood a magnificent sea-shell shaped like a trumpet in which stuck six artificial red poppies. The cups and saucers were heavily patterned with flowers and the tea-pot was of lustre and of great value though neither the owners nor the guests knew it. By each plate lay a paper table napkin with a deep border of purple violets. The sea-shell was flanked by dishes on every side. One held a gigantic red lobster, another green water cress, a third a great mound of bramble jelly and the fourth held a rich, lardy cake generously buttered. Piles of fresh bread and butter were also provided and ladder-back chairs black with age were placed ready for the guests.

The B.B. made itself "at home" with the greatest delight though at Rainbow End lobster, fresh bread and lardy cake never appeared and if they had the Professor and Mrs. Bly would never have enjoyed the claws with such joyful *abandon* as their host and hostess. The tea was strong, sweet and slightly smoky; the jelly was marvellous, but the best part of the feast was the conversation which was as rich and varied as the fare.

They learnt that Mrs. Jeans' grandmother had walked six miles to school every day, had never heard of a school-bus, and always had to pass a gibbet where the bones of dead men rattled in the wood.

Sam Jeans had run away to sea at the age of eight; had been wrecked and lashed to a spar in a raging storm for twenty-four hours before he was rescued by Chinese pirates. Both Sam and Kate constantly saw "ghostses" and stated that the wooden mermaid in the corner always played her lyre on Christmas Eve at midnight.

They were listening to these entrancing tales when a sharp whistle sounded and Sam gulped down his fifth cup of tea, wiped his lobstery hands on the table-cloth, scorning the paper napkins, and made for the door which was shut tightly because Mr. and Mrs. Jeans liked to eat without a lot of tiresome fresh air making them uncomfortable.

"That'll be the gent from London," said Mrs. Jeans complacently, "maybe Sam'll bring him up for a bite."

"But what does he want Mr. Jeans for?"

"To row him over to his boat, miss . . . he often sleeps aboard even when he is not sailing her."

"Oh, Mrs. Jeans . . . could we see them start?" asked Georgie.

"When we've helped clear away you mean," said Jacky, who knew by experience that a disagreeable duty called washing-up always came after a feast.

"Bless you, miss . . . I'll soon clear away the things! You go along and enjoy yerselves."

But Jacky insisted she must be helped and it really

was rather fun washing up in a tin basin on a bench while Mrs. Jeans was made to sit on her rocking chair and continue her exciting tales about battle and murder and sudden death.

Afterwards they rushed to the shore where Sam and the London gent were sitting in the boat smoking.

"Young ladies from the new school," said Sam briefly with a wave of his pipe towards the new arrivals and the "gent" bowed politely.

He was young, dressed in shabby grey flannels and a jersey and Jacky liked his smile.

"I thought young ladies at school went about two and two with a schoolmistress bringing up the rear," he said. "Have you escaped or what?"

"We've been having tea with Mrs. Jeans and ours isn't that sort of school, thank goodness."

"What names do you answer to?"

"I'm Jack—this is Georgie, that's Jerry and this one is Bert."

"Oh, I see." He gave an understanding twinkle and said "Well, I'm Bill, pleased to meet you."

Jack, George, Jerry and Bert returned the compliment.

"Would you like to row over and see my little packet?"

"We should *love* it." They all spoke at once and he seemed pleased at the rapture in their faces.

"Right you are. Let's push off, Sam."

Sam pushed off and the passengers waded through the surf and boarded the *Seabird* and were soon rocking over the waves to the little yacht.

La Belle Dame was a "lovely lady" but did not show that ship-shape trimness that usually marks a privately owned yacht; in fact she needed a coat of paint badly.

As the *Seabird* came alongside a red head appeared above them and a boy of about sixteen shouted, "Coming aboard, sir?"

"Ay, ay," shouted Bill, and the four girls began to enjoy themselves with all their might because they thought only people in sea stories really said "Ay, ay."

The boy let down a ladder and Bill went up and the guests followed. The decks might have been cleaner and there was a litter of ropes, sails, anchors and shipping gear lying about and Bill shouted to Steve, the boy, that he deserved a rope end.

"Is Steve the crew?" enquired Jacky.

"He wants to be—but he'll have to mend his ways if he is to bring it off—but never mind him, now. Come and look at my lovely lady and excuse her untidy appearance, please gentlemen. Go down the companion steps into my snug dug-out."

Descending the companion-way they found themselves in a cosy little cabin painted white, the seats covered with blue mattresses. A small stove stood on a lead sheet and a lamp in a swinging frame hung over a fixed square table. There was cupboards in the walls, a shelf of books and a map of France pinned above it.

"Is she a French boat?" asked George.

"She's French built and English owned."

"What do you call this part?" asked Jacky.

"We are amidships now—that's the private part of a ship, you know, but this leads to the galley."

Bill opened a door into a narrow passage with sleeping bunks on one side for the crew and a tiny kitchen on the other. Another door led to the men's quarters and the sail lockers.

Bill answered all questions without a trace of that amused patronage the experienced sea-goer so often shows to the ignorant land-lubber. He then led them back into the cabin and opening a cupboard said, "I see you are all bent on going to sea some day so you had better get used to ship rations" and he served out a ship's biscuit all round, as hard as stone but alluringly romantic.

"Has it got weevils in it?" asked Georgie, who had read a great many eighteenth-century sea stories and Jerry and Bert threw theirs down with stifled shrieks and Jacky plodded through hers and accused the B.B. of unmanliness.

This led to an explanation of the new society and George produced a rather grubby copy of the Rules.

Bill studied it with an interest that was flattering, "Seems all right to me, but I don't see why young ladies need to be young gentlemen and I don't like *Rule IV*—societies *ought* to be secret."

"Oh, that's exactly what we think," cried three members of the B.B.

"I gather the idea is to do good by stealth?" asked Bill. "No flag-waving, bands, or medals but just making a good thing of some job as they do in the Secret Service?"

This seemed an attractive way of putting it and Jacky heaved a sigh of relief for her conscience constantly pricked her about the B.B.

"Yes," she said, "I suppose that is the idea, but what I meant about being open and above board is that I'll never be a party to getting into silly, schoolgirl scrapes which the Professor and Mrs. Bly would hate . . . they've been jolly decent to me."

Bill stared at her curiously and said, "Are you the captain?"

"I suppose I am."

"What would you think of letting yourself and your men get some expert knowledge—according to *Rule II* —of sailing? I don't mind taking you out sometimes in my 'lovely lady'."

"But that would be *scrumptious* . . . when?"

"Does the schoolmistress always let you go about in this unattached way?"

"We are fairly free, but we can't do *exactly* as we like. To-day we had leave to come and visit Mrs. Jeans who cooks for us."

"Then I'll give a message to Mrs. Jeans when I can take you sailing and leave you to arrange the rest."

"Thanks *most* awfully . . . we'd simply *love* it!"

The B.B. liked their host more and more every moment.

"So would I—I'm fond of boys. By the way, where is this rummy school of yours?"

"About a mile from here . . . it's a camp on the cliffs."

"Do you pass Farley's farm?"

"Not exactly, but we go quite near to it."

"Would it get you into a 'silly schoolgirl scrape' if you stopped there and gave Farley a message from me?"

"Of course not."

"That's nice of you—I can't trust Steve and Sam's afraid of the watch-dog."

"What shall we say?"

"Ask for Farley and say . . . Mr. Bill Briggs is going for a short cruise on Saturday, but he'll be back in time to give a hand with the hay-ricks."

"Yes, we'll tell him, and now I'm afraid we have to go, please."

Sam was hauled out of the fo'csle where he was having a hot argument with Steve and the guests said goodbye to Bill and descended the ladder and were rowed back to shore to say "thank you" to Mrs. Jeans.

On the way home Jacky discovered that she was more popular than ever and the B.B. an enormous success. It was entirely through her making friends with Mrs. Jeans that they were invited to the Black Cottage which led to an acquaintance who owned a yacht.

"If you think I was nice to Mrs. Jeans because of the Black Cottage, you are jolly well mistaken," said Jacky. "I always make friends with people who are kind enough to do the dirty work for us because it's up to us to show we are grateful. After all, George was decent to me when I was a new cook in the first place." She flashed a smile at Georgie, who blushed with pleasure.

Farley's Farm stood back from the sea up a winding lane and they had never actually visited it. It was a rambling place with endless sheds and barns and as they approached the farmyard a large black dog began to bark furiously as it leapt on its chain.

"If it gets free it will certainly kill us," said Bert. "I'm not surprised Sam isn't fond of calling here."

A man came out of a barn and stared at them.

"Please, are you Mr. Farley?" asked Jacky.

"Yes, I'm Farley—is there anything amiss?" He looked suspicious.

"Oh, no, but we've brought a message. Mr. Bill Briggs is going for a short cruise on Saturday, but he will be back in time to give a hand with the hay ricks."

The man gave them a hard stare and then, rather surprisingly, for they were now used to hearing the simple Dorset dialect of the country people he answered,

"Thank you, miss . . . that will be O.K. by me."

CHAPTER VII

"LA BELLE DAME"

JACKY had criticised Rainbow End for its no rules system but she was as chagrined as the rest of the B.B. when a special rule was now made entirely for their benefit.

The Professor—greatly distressed—and Mrs. Bly, conventional for once, said with great determination that on no account could any of their pupils go sailing in the bay with a complete stranger, and they were much perturbed that four of them had already visited the yacht without leave.

"And serve you all right, too," said Cecilia and Audrey when the girls appeared in their tent to air their grievances. "The man might be a murderer."

"Rubbish!" The B.B. were scornful. "He's jolly nice."

"Murderers often are . . . it is the way they get their victims, and remember, girls, no getting away with it on the sly. We are supposed to be responsible for you, but we expect you to be responsible for yourselves."

Jacky shrugged her shoulders. "If you mean me, I don't do things 'on the sly' or go about with people who do. I think the rule is silly but if it's made it has to be kept and that's the end of it."

To calm things down the Professor decided to be what the girls called "cricket-mad." Bats, balls, cricket pads, and stumps all arrived at Rainbow End and everyone was expected to be as enthusiastic as he was himself. Even Mrs. Bly was expected to play and Doris was urged to finish her work early and Mrs. Jeans, chuckling and breathless, was persuaded to field. The Professor, whose top score in his college days was 126 felt capable of anything and sent home for his old cap and blazer which gave a professional air to the proceedings and impressed beginners. Nothing but first-class cricket was any good to the Professor and to achieve it the teams must constantly practise. Walks became unpopular and folk-dancing and Greek posturing was almost forgotten. The Professor also lost interest in fossil-hunts for the time being and Sally Parker and Ethel Forbes, who were keen and had hoped to find the remains of some prehistoric beast and become famous were inclined to complain until the Professor praised their bowling and from that moment they became cricket enthusiasts. Jacky, well-trained by her step-father was a good all-round player and her batting delighted the Professor.

The B.B. in consequence, panted to excel, and though Miss Lyle remained calm and detached Miss Carroll became almost as fanatical as the Captain of the team.

The weather was perfect, the encampment remaining cool by the sea breezes, though inland the heat was almost tropical.

Everyone was as brown as a berry and everyone seemed happy, even the complaining Ethel, whom one could not expect even cricket to turn into a charming personality all at once, improved vastly and was now seldom rude to Jacky.

Jacky's own face had lost the anxious look which had so much distressed the Professor, but she still indulged in silent weeps about her strange position in the school and had awful forbodings about the time when the camp must break up and return to London. She hoped and prayed that Dick would make his fortune quickly and send for her to join him. She had a dreadful feeling that if this did not happen that she and the hens and Billy Slowboy and the Japanese prints would once more have to face a cold world.

One day Georgie said to her, "Everything is nice and jolly, but the term is flying and I do wish the B.B. could have another adventure . . . what a sell it is we can't learn sailing."

"As a matter of fact the rule hasn't made any difference to that . . . Bill has never asked us and Mrs. Jeans says they haven't seen him for a fortnight. What on earth is the matter, Felicity?"

Felicity, who had adored Jacky from the first and was often considered a nuisance by the B.B. appeared with Ethel at the tent door in floods of tears.

"Cato is lost!"

"Lost . . . why he was cadging milk at breakfast-time."

"Yes, but he went off after that and Doris saw him

go off in the gorse bushes. That's hours ago and I've called and called.''

Cato had taken to open-air life and though he pursued rabbits occasionally and often rambled he always came back to meals and to occupy his favourite bed in the caravan.

"Well don't cry . . . we'll *all* call. Come along girls.''

"But Jacky, we were going to bathe before supper.''

"Well, that's off as far as I'm concerned . . . but don't mind me.''

But, for some reason Jacky always had a following and the two girls came too, calling out to Bert: " We are going cat-hunting.''

"Doris's aunt had a cat once who went down a rabbit-hole and never came up again—suffocated,'' said Ethel morbidly, and Felicity's sobs increased.

"Don't be such a little idiot!'' Jacky frowned at Ethel who said, " Why are you always so down on me? It's true.''

"Doris *would* tell you that, of course, and I suppose Mrs. Jeans said Cato was drowned or carried off by a seagull? We will all go in different directions and call as we go . . . but you stick to me, Felicity.''

There were always rabbits on the grassy down and among the gorse bushes and Jacky suspected Cato had gone hunting.

Suddenly Ethel's voice was heard crying, "Oh, the poor little thing!'' and she was discovered standing over a furry rabbit lying dead with its head in a snare.

"I bet that's what happened to Cato,'' muttered Jerry.

"I say, Felicity, suppose you run home and see if

he has come back?" suggested Jacky, but Felicity sobbing wildly refused to leave them and they went on their way pouncing on any snares they saw.

"Hush! Oh, do be quiet . . . can't you hear?" Felicity stood still and they all heard a cat mewing.

"Don't call," said Jacky hastily, "and don't rush . . . we mustn't frighten him."

They advanced cautiously into an open clearing where close to a gorse bush sat Cato gazing intently before him.

"*Quiet*, please." Jacky went forward quietly and swiftly and knelt down beside the cat whose neck was in a snare so tightly that the slightest struggle would have strangled him.

"Come here, Ethel, please, and hold him." Although afraid of the snare and that she would be scratched, Ethel, immensely flattered to be chosen over the heads of Jacky's special chums came forward and held Cato firmly while Jacky pulled the wire over his head and set him free. He immediately started for home at full pelt with Felicity after him and Ethel, too.

"Did you ever see such a clever little beast? He sat stone-still till help came."

"And yet he's a town cat."

"Doris's aunt's cat must have been a brainless idiot."

"Why on earth did you call Ethel to help?" Georgie seemed indignant.

"Because she had been decent to Felicity about Cato and showed some pity for that poor strangled rabbit. She's evidently got a heart somewhere."

"What a queer lad, you are, Jack." The B.B. regarded her affectionately and Jerry said, "I should never have thought of looking for Ethel's heart, but if she really has got one and stops giggling and being cheeky, good luck to her . . . I say, *do* look over there!"

"It's *La Belle Dame* . . . at anchor!"

On the distant sea they could see Bill Brigg's "Lovely Lady" gently rocking on the waves and Bert was rushing up the steps from the beach with the news.

Someone else came up the steps, too, a tall figure in grey flannels with his hands in his pockets.

"It's Bill!" cried Georgie. "Do you think he can possibly be coming to call on the Professor and Bee so that we can all be properly introduced? Won't it be too spiffing if he is and they find out he isn't a murderer at all."

"And then he'll probably ask Cecilia and Audrey to go sailing with him instead of us," said Jerry, gloomily, "or Miss Carroll and Miss Lyle, he'll think they are 'nice young ladies'."

"He *is* coming here," called out Bert. "Oh Jacky . . . don't you ever get excited?"

Jacky laughed. "Of course I do. I'm terribly excited and I want to go sailing most awfully. Let's go and meet him and get first innings before he has a chance to ask Cecilia and Audrey."

They arrived at the steps as Bill reached the top and stood gazing at the encampment in astonishment.

"Hallo! How are you, my hearties?"

"Splendid. How are you, Bill?"

"Only so-so . . . I say, you said this was a *school*!"

"Well, so it is."

"But where are the schoolmistresses and the black-boards and the canes?"

"The schoolmistresses are on the veranda reading.

That's the schoolmaster over there practising bowling,
and we don't have blackboards or canes."

" I've come to call on the schoolmaster—will he talk
to me in Latin?"

" No, he'll ask you if you can bowl! It is jolly you
have come because we are all broken-hearted about the
sailing."

" I've come to arrange that, too."

" But they think you are a kidnapper or a
murderer!"

"Gosh! Never mind, I'll settle 'em. Is there a front
door and a bell, or do I crawl into one of these tents on
my hands and knees and salaam?"

Full of mirth the B.B. lead him to the Professor and
introduced him as " Mr. Bill Briggs, the gentleman we
met at Mrs. Jeans' tea party."

The Professor beamed. He had entirely forgotten
all the arguments about this villain's invitation to go
sailing and he was glad to see a man after some weeks
of schoolgirls and he said, " Glad to see you, my dear
sir . . . you are a cricketer, I feel sure?"

Within five minutes Bill was batting and the
Professor bowling and every girl available, Miss
Carroll, Miss Lyle and even Mrs. Bly and Doris were
fielding wildly. The innings ended and Bill was
conducted to the Chief's tent where the Chieftainess
joined them with a tray of cool drinks. She was grati-
fied to learn that he thought Rainbow End a paradise
for young people, and invited them all to come and see
his yacht in turn in parties of six the next day. Then
he took his leave after further endearing himself to the
Professor by saying he was interested in geology.

The B.B. accompanied him to the steps and learnt

with joy that permission had actually been given for all four of them to go for a short cruise in *La Belle Dame* the following Saturday.

"Be at Sam's at nine sharp and he'll row you out."

In the wildest spirits Georgie, and Jerry and Bert rushed home to supper and Jacky was left alone with Bill. He looked at her keenly, "Had any adventures yet, Captain?"

"No, worse luck! . . . can't think of a thing."

They grinned at each other with complete understanding.

"Look here—I'll help you out and think of some plan on Saturday and if you agree it will give 'em something to keep them quiet!"

"Thanks awfully, Bill. You see really I'm all for a quiet life and peace; but ever since I arrived here they seem to think I'm a gangster or something and look to me for some excitement."

"Well, we'll show 'em . . . so long, Jack, I'll see you on Saturday."

It was maddening to see parties being rowed over to *La Belle Dame* the next day; but a relief, when they returned full of enthusiasm for the yacht and its skipper, to hear nobody except the B.B. had been invited to cruise in her.

The next day Bill came for cricket again and did some excellent training in fielding which he declared needed brains.

"You ought to arrange a match with the village team," he suggested. "It's a jolly good one, I hear."

"We've watched it . . . it's almost pro."

"All the better . . . show you your weak spots."

"Would they deign to notice us?" asked Miss Lyle,

who loved competition and thought life dull without it.

"I know a chap named Farley whose grandson is in it and I'll ask him. Practise for all you are worth the next fortnight. Jacintha's bowling is really decent but you need better all-round team work and do tell that girl you call Doris not to yell when she sees the ball coming towards her but to keep her wits about her and catch it."

"Oh, Doris is keen enough," said Miss Lyle, "but she can never quite realise she is not playing rounders."

Saturday was a perfect day and the party arrived at the Black cottage long before nine. Sam was there mending lobster-pots and said he didn't see no reason why they shouldn't go aboard at once as Mr. Briggs wasn't a gent that took offence. As they rowed towards the yacht the sun was shining on the water and the distant coast line seemed to fade away in the mists which Sam said meant a fine day.

"Boat ahoy!" shouted Sam as they drew alongside and there was Bill, looking more naval than usual in a white yachting cap and coat. The crew—Steve—was more presentable, too, and pulled a forelock as he let down the ladder for the guests and offered them a helping hand.

The decks were clear of litter and when they reached the cabin they found a pot of pink geraniums, a dish of cherries and a box of chocolate creams laid out tastefully. They were urged to take refreshment immediately.

Bill said he would leave them with the chocolate creams while he went and got his "Lovely Lady" going.

"Bill . . . could *we* be the crew . . . just for the day?"

"Well, I thought that was the idea? Signed on for a short cruise along the west coast, haven't you? I've sent Steve ashore for the day off and I'll want men for his jobs."

"Oh *jolly* . . . I'll be first mate because I spoke first," said Georgie.

"Now then, George . . . you can't have all the plums. You fellows had better draw lots for ship's duties." Bill took four slips of paper, wrote on them, shook them in his cap and invited Jacky to pick one.

She did so with excitement and to her dismay drew . . . *cook*!

"Just my luck! I hoped I'd be cabin-boy."

"Well, anyhow, you know your job," comforted Georgie.

Georgie came next and drew "cabin-boy," and Jerry followed with "first mate" and Bert ended with "boatswain."

"What does the first mate do?"

"He is the skipper's right hand and if I'm washed overboard you'll have to carry on. And you keep your eye on the ship's crew and see that the hands do their job and all work for the welfare of the ship."

"I'll jolly well make them work! Now then Jack— what are you loitering there for, man . . . get off to the galley and do your job."

"And what does the boatswain do?"

"Anything the mate tells him . . . and the cabin-boy is a sort of fag at everyone's beck and call. Now then, lads, all hands on deck, we are going to raise the anchor and get her going."

Bill was deadly serious and so were his crew. They burned to become perfect seamen and so eager were

they to learn that after half-an-hour never again would
the first mate call a ship's sheets " ropes " and was soon
speaking glibly of halyards, jibs, and foresails and was
grumbling at the cabin-boy, too, for calling *La Belle
Dame* a yacht like a land-lubber, instead of alluding to
her as a ship or a boat.

How marvellous it was to be sailing at last towards
the open sea leaving behind them Old Harry and his
wife, two chalky cliffs guarding the entrance to
Swanage. The seagulls were whirling overhead and the
wind was tugging at the rigging and the crew crowded
round the skipper at the helm. They hugged the coast-
line at first; the bit of English coast that grows in beauty
and grandeur and varied colour as it wanders on to the
west. The jagged, rocky cliffs of Swanage were like
huge, bastion walls and between them were the green
fissures of the chines, small coves, inlets, and sometimes the shores were golden with sand or shingly, with
caves behind looking as if they held smugglers' secrets.

Bill seemed to know the coast as well as he knew his
own name and his tales of this land in the old days were
as good as Mrs. Jeans only less morbid. Leaving
Swanage the coast line becomes wilder, sandy beaches
disappeared and rocky, sinister heights rose straight
from the sea.

"That's Dancing Ledge," shouted the skipper
pointing to a flat slab of rock sloping like a wide,
smooth shelf down to the roaring sea.

"Where? Where? Who dances there?" The crew
rushed to look.

"I haven't a notion . . . sea fiends, I should think."

"It looks frightfully dangerous and I can't imagine
Bee wanting us to do folk-dancing there," said

Georgie, and Bert added, "I do hate, those black, small bits of rock . . . they look so sinister. I love the chalky white bits with the gleams of gold and red."

"That, my dear child," said Georgie in the Professor's manner, "is caused by the deeper sections of strata. Have we not already learnt that the Dorset formations belong largely to the oolitic where there is a species of granular limestone . . . take a note of that, child."

"Oh do be quiet, I've no intention of becoming an 'expert' in geology, though I'd like to find another *Ichthyosaurus Platydin* in the cliffs."

"Did you ever hear of St. Aldhelm . . . we'll get a good view of his head in a few minutes," said Bill. "He was a geologist."

"I thought he was a saint?"

"So he was, but lots of saints had hobbies and he knew all about Portland Stone and that's a kind of oolitic. He once told some workmen to dig for a treasure and the treasure turned out to be Portland Stone."

"How jolly . . . I wonder if the Professor knows? If he doesn't he'll be impressed and let us come sailing with you again." Georgie industriously made a note.

"What's that building on the top of the Headland?"

"St. Aldhelm's Chapel. In the old days before lighthouses were invented a cresset of flames was lit there every night to guide the fishermen home . . . and I bet it guided a few pirates home, too."

"Where are we making for, Skipper?"

"You'll see . . . we've a call to make . . . and look here, mate, oughtn't that cook to be doing his job?"

George said, "Look here, Jack, you didn't sign on to

sprawl over the deck. Get down to the galley and make a spotted Dick or a sea-pie or something."

" Oh well, I can't see why we can't live on fresh air on a lovely day like this," grumbled Jacky, but she got up and sauntered towards the galley.

Her methodical mind took pleasure in the way it was arranged. Rows of pots and pans, all evidently cleaned up for the occasion, were on the shelves and canisters and tins contained a plentiful supply of food Fresh bread, rolls and cakes were in the bread pan, milk and butter in coolers, potatoes were already peeled in a jar and tomatoes and lettuce set ready for a salad. She decided she needn't cook at all, but would open a large tin of tongue, slice it and serve it with a salad and the potatoes could be fried. Tinned apricots and custard could follow and if they didn't like it they could find another cook.

How jolly it was sailing on the open sea with sea breezes coming in through the tiny port-hole as she worked. For the moment Jacky decided to try and forget her worries; the term flying and a time to face when she would once again be a pupil who couldn't pay her school fees.

She could hear they were having an uproarious time on deck, for the Skipper was letting everyone have a turn at the tiller and explaining the watch.

She thought it was about time the cabin-boy did his job, too, and she called him to lay the cloth in the cabin. Georgie came reluctantly; but found the galley so fascinating she called the bo'sun and the mate and Jacky left them all to investigate and went on deck for a breather and to take the Skipper his lunch. It ended by them all coming on deck for their meal sitting

in the sun near the Skipper who asked if they would
like to hear the story of his life

"Rather . . . but don't let it be *too* exciting or I
shall forget to fetch the fried potatoes," said Jacky.

"Do you know, my lads, why I 'took to you,' as
Mrs. Jeans would say, when I first met you?"

"No, do tell us."

"It was because of that secret society of yours—the
B.B."

"But why "

"Well, you see . . . can you keep a dead secret?"

"*Of course.*" The answer was unanimous.

"Can you be as silent as Davy Jones's Locker?"

"Ay, ay, Skipper."

"Cross your hearts." They crossed their hearts.

"Now we have got rid of Steve and are together on the
ocean waves where nobody can hear us I should like to
tell you *I am in the Secret Service.*"

There was dead silence for a minute; three of the
girls regarding Bill with awe, Jacky, a little startled at
first then secretly amused. Bill certainly was helping
her to provide a thrill for the B.B. She had always
been struck by their lack of brains, and here they were
again taking all this in with the utmost seriousness.

"Oh, Bill. How *frightfully* exciting!" Georgie
gasped, and the cabin-boy and the bo'sun seemed
almost speechless.

"And is *La Belle Dame* in the secret service, too?"

Jacky asked this question and looked teasingly at
Bill who returned it with a seriousness which puzzled
her. Surely he could not possibly mean it.

"Yes, my 'Lovely Lady' is a modern girl and all
out for adventure. That's why she is not looking as

smart as most French ladies. I don't take her into the harbour because we don't want to draw attention to ourselves."

"And what do you *do* . . . please tell us!"

"Agents of the S.S. don't talk about what they *do*. All the same, as you are all members of a sort of secret society, too, and I can see you are honest lads, I'm going to ask you to help me."

The first mate, the bo'sun and the cabin-boy could hardly believe their ears; in their wildest dream of adventure they had never dreamt they could ever be in the confidence of an S.S. agent.

The ship's cook gazed intently at them all; but they ignored her.

"But what do we do . . . and when?"

"You do what I tell you . . . this very afternoon, I've got important documents to deliver that may not go through the post safely and cannot be carried over land without great risk. *We are being watched.*"

"Do you mean we are suspected?"

"Not specially . . . but all sea craft is watched, that's why we have to be careful where we land."

"Oh, are we going to *land*?"

"We are . . . but first, aren't we going to have any more grub?"

"Ay, ay, sir."

The crew all tumbled to the galley to fetch the fried potatoes and the apricots, all gloriously happy for so far, the day was surpassing their expectations.

"You *might* have made a spotted Dick," said Georgie reproachfully.

"It's too hot for suet, but if we are befogged or anything like that I'll knock you up a sea-pie for supper."

"I wonder who Bill will choose to carry the despatches and whether we will have to protect them with our lives?"

"It seems a rummy idea to come to sea to despatch them on the land," Jacky laughed.

"I expect we shall have to draw lots. But if you and I are chosen promise me you won't make me giggle if a coast-watcher holds us up?" Georgie requested.

"I'm going to take the Skipper the rest of his grub . . . you can finish yours down here." Jacky departed, determined to get to the bottom of Bill's wild proposals.

He greeted her with pleasure and let her take the tiller while he smoked a cigarette.

"I say, Bill, you won't land us into a scrape, will you? I'm not a parlour boarder at Rainbow End and I can't afford to risk being there when the other parlour boarders are run in for carrying secret despatches."

"Don't dare to tell me you are not enjoying yourself, Jack?"

"Of course I am . . . it's a gorgeous day, but I'd like to know your real plan and *need* we land?"

"We jolly well need to land and all you and those precious innocents making all that noise midships have to do is to do what you are told."

There was a rush on to the deck and the precious innocents arrived anxiously.

"What are you talking about? I believe Jacky knows more than we do and it isn't fair."

"I don't know a thing except the cabin-boy has to wash-up. I'm going to stretch myself on a bunk. Cooks always do after dinner."

And in spite of Georgie's protests Jacky did retire to one of the bunks in the sleeping quarters and read one of the sea yarns she found on the bookshelf, while the first mate and the bo'sun quarrelled about who should take the tiller. She was just enjoying a thrilling chapter when the first mate called down and said they were under the shelter if St. Aldhelm's Head and the Skipper was going to land.

CHAPTER VIII

THE JOLLY MARINERS

WHEN Jacky came on deck she saw they were at anchor close to a little cove under the shelter of St. Aldhelm's great head. It was a gentle little bit of coast-line with black cliffs and green downs above and a sandy beach below where lay old tarred boat-houses, huts, fishing-tackle, lobster-pots and a very ancient-looking boat, and the remains of a battered old pier nearly washed away by the sea. The cove seemed deserted except for one fisherman lazily tarring a boat in the sunshine.

"What a queer little place!"

"It's the place where all the old fishing-boats are sent to die. You can see 'em lying there with their timbers fast becoming skeletons!" The B.B. shivered, for the old boats really did look weird and the dark cliffs and the loneliness of the shore a little sinister.

"But we don't want to visit the ghosts of ships," Jacky objected. "We would rather go on sailing in the sun."

"All the same . . . we've got to land, mates."

Bill leaned over the bulwarks; put his hand to his mouth and shouted: "Ship Ahoy!" and the fisherman looked up and put down his tar-brush and came down to the water's edge where a boat lay rocking.

"Do you know him?"

"Yes . . . but don't expect to get any fun out of him . . . he's dumb. Now we must make ready, come below, mates," Bill led the wondering B.B. down below to the forecastle and opened a locker. Inside there were four good-sized knapsacks of the kind used by hikers.

"Here are the despatches."

"*What!*" The B.B. could hardly believe their eyes or their ears.

"They *can't* be." Georgie looked incredulous. "I thought secret despatches had to be hidden about your person and made so small that one could eat them if danger threatened them!"

"Not always. These happen to be particularly bulky despatches . . . that's why I am asking for your valuable help."

"What do we do with them?" Jacky glared at Bill as she thought he was testing the credulity of the " precious innocents" too far, but he refused to meet her eye.

"You fasten them on . . . like this." Bill strapped the knapsacks on their shoulders and they discovered they were remarkably heavy.

"And you just look like what you are . . . school-girls going off for a short hike inland as you are a little tired of yachting with your uncle Bill."

"Remember we are not going to tell any lies."

"No need for that, captain—don't be alarmed, I'm not really a wicked uncle. The boat man will land you

and you all march straight up that sandy lane in front
of you until you come to a sign-post which says
Durdlecombe. Keep straight on again——"

"How far?"

"About half-a-mile—till you come to a little inn and
a few thatched cottages. The inn is called The Jolly
Mariners and that's your destination."

"Do you mean *you* are not coming, too?" Jacky
demanded.

"My dear chap—certainly not—I want it to look like
a little schoolgirl excursion. You march up to The
Jolly Mariners and ask if you can have tea."

"*That* at least will be jolly," said Bert.

"You will be asked if you prefer to have it in the
parlour or in the garden and the answer is: *The parlour, if we can have it to ourselves.* That's the pass-
word."

The B.B. began to cheer up again and Jacky shrugged her shoulders. "What will happen then?"

"The landlord will take you to the parlour and say,
'Is there any news of my friend, Mr. Briggs?' and you
answer 'Mr. Briggs sends his compliments and will you
please supply the stores as usual?' You then hand
over the knapsacks and bring back what he gives you."

"Will it be more despatches?"

"Good gracious, no . . . something much nicer.
Come straight back when you have had tea."

"Do we pay for the tea?"

"No, that's all right and they'll do you well. The
boat will be waiting to row you back here . . . so off
you go."

It didn't seem any use protesting, besides, as Georgie
pointed out later they had asked for it, and things

promised to be exciting as they descended the ladder to the waiting boat, Bill's last words being: "Good luck, and remember I trust you to deliver the goods."

"Ay, ay, Skipper." The B.B. tried to look sporting.

The little cove was the oddest place and it seemed as if it were not only a place where old boats came to die but a graveyard for all sea things. Windlasses, rotten cables, old anchors lay half-buried in the sand and from the shattered timbers of old boats sea-grass sprang in green patches. If the boatman had not been dumb he would probably have told them that these things were relics of the days when Frenchmen hoped to make a fortune out of Dorset shale, and the abandoned shipping-gear was all that was left of their failure to do so.

The B.B. smiled their thanks at the dumb boatman and surveyed the land. The sandy lane was in a cleft of the cliffs and they set out to climb up at once wishing that the sun was less hot and Bill's secret despatches less heavy.

"Perhaps they are bombs," suggested Bert, but Georgie thought they were more likely to be docu ments concerning secrets about atom bombs. Their feet sank into the hot sand and the sun blazed down on their loaded backs.

"I must say," groaned Georgie, "I never knew before that S.S. agents gave their dirty work for some one else to do."

"But don't pretend you are not enjoying doing some dirty work," admonished Jacky. "You wanted something thrilling to do."

"I'm sure we've walked miles," said Jerry. "I say, suppose Bill *is* a murderer and we are all walking into a trap."

Bert, not so keen on adventure as the others, went a little pale and Jacky said, "Don't be silly, please."

"There's the sign-post," cried Georgie, pointing to the finger-post at the top of the lane which read *To Durdlecombe.*

They trudged on again until they reached a group of thatched cottages looking as deserted as the distant cove and not far from there stood the inn, a low, white building also thatched, with benches outside and small tables.

A sign hung over the door proclaiming it The Jolly Mariners and below it they read, *John Lillywhite, licensed to sell spirits and tobacco.* A woman was sitting outside knitting and Jacky marched up boldly and said, "Could we have tea, please?"

"That you can, miss. Will 'ee take it outside or in the parlour?"

"The parlour, if we can have it to ourselves, please," answered Jacky and immediately a man in a white apron—plainly "John Lillywhite," the innkeeper, came out of a little bar and said, "Good afternoon, little ladies . . . any news of Mr. Briggs?"

Greatly resenting being called a "little lady" Jacky, as instructed by Bill, answered rather haughtily.

."That's right . . . come right in and take off them heavy bags and set ye down and rest and the missus will set ye tea in a jiffy."

The inn parlour seemed almost too good to be true, and every jolly mariner in the Seven Seas must have contributed something to its ornamentation. So low that their heads almost bumped upon the beams it was also exceedingly dark, but refreshingly cool after the hot sunshine. Model ships of every description in glass cases, and ships in bottles, decorated the broad oak ledges all round the room. Between them and on the high chimney-piece there were enormous shells from the South Seas, great lumps of coral, fossilised sponges, birds' eggs, blown out and hanging on strings and frightful to behold, a squid bottled in spirits. On a side table loaded with curiosities from the deep stood a huge ship's bell. The pictures on the walls were all sea subjects, too, mostly of wrecks with the frantic survivors clinging to rafts and spars.

"I should think the jolliest jolly mariner in the world would get the dumps here," remarked Jacky.

"I do wish I had said we would take tea in the garden—that squid is enough to take away anyone's appetite."

"Don't look at it. I say, isn't it bliss to get rid of these . . . you know *what*?" Georgie rubbed her aching shoulders, thinking it would be indiscreet for an S.S. agent to speak the word "despatches" in an inn-parlour.

"And what on earth does a man like John Lilly-white have to do with the Queen's despatches," asked Bert, who was not discreet.

"Dad says that it was the marvellous methods of the S.S. that won the war," said Jerry, "so I suppose it's all right. I wonder what they will give us for tea?"

"Squid, probably." Georgie looked at Jacky maliciously. "Anyhow I hope it isn't lobster, my appetite feels delicate."

At that moment Mrs. Lillywhite came bustling in with a tea-tray and flung on the table a white cloth on which she set cups, saucers, plates and a huge jug of thick cream.

There was a dish of fresh strawberries, too, home-made bread, scones, split and filled with raspberry jam and cream and a china hen containing a pile of boiled eggs.

"Oh, Mrs. Lillywhite . . . what a scrumptious tea!"

"I hope you'll all enjoy it, miss, I'm sure . . . Mr. Briggs said to get something nice for four young ladies and I thought them strawberries would tempt 'ee like."

"I should think they *will*!" They began the feast at once, Jacky with her back to the squid. Mrs. Lillywhite, who, unlike Mrs. Jeans, seemed reluctant to talk, went out of the room assuring them there was plenty more of everything.

They ate as only schoolgirls can and refreshed and cooled, in spite of a great many cups of boiling tea, screwed up their courage, for nobody appeared, to make a timid onslaught on the ship's bell.

John Lillywhite appeared with the knapsacks.

"Well, ladies. I hope the missus gave 'ee what 'ee liked?"

"It was all perfectly lovely."

"That's right . . . us don't want to starve folk that comes out to Durdlecombe . . . now here's bags with the things for Mr. Briggs. He be rare fond of a bit o' good butter and farm stuff and tell 'im Lillywhite's always ready for the bags."

Mr. Lillywhite was certainly a most amazing S.S. agent and treated the whole matter of the despatches as if they had been a present of fresh lobster from Bill, which he was returning by some farm produce. "The precious innocents" were completely at sea and Jacky a little annoyed. It was most kind of Bill of course to plan this sort of adventure which the B.B. had completely accepted as a real one, and the tea had been lovely; but she would rather have been cruising on the cool sea, or even planning cricket triumphs at Rainbow End.

The B.B. promised to give the message and thanking their host again for their tea they saw they were now expected to take their departure; probably because spies were loitering round the inn. So they said good-bye to The Jolly Mariners and its landlord and started on their return journey.

"I do wish he had asked us to look round," sighed Georgie. "Except for the tea I don't call it frightfully exciting carrying despatches, and not a bit like descriptions of it in books."

"George . . . what an ass you are." Jacky gave a grin which turned into a look of stolid indifference when a man on a bicycle appeared in the sandy lane. He was in naval uniform and when he reached them he dismounted and said, "Excuse me, young ladies, but if you are on a hike this lane leads right to the shore and you can't get beyond with the tide coming in."

"Thank you very much but we are heading for the cove to join our ship," Jacky answered him, and the others looked at her in consternation for surely S.S. agents should not tell complete strangers their destination; especially as Bill said so plainly that he wanted them to impersonate hikers.

"Oh, so you are yachtswomen?" He looked at the knapsack with silent amusement and Bert, who had been nervous all along, felt her knees shake. Supposing he asked to see the contents of their knapsacks in the Queen's name and Mr. Lillywhite had put more secret despatches cosily among the butter and bacon?

"Yes . . . we are cruising round with a friend and we've been to fetch some ship's stores from Durdle-combe."

How clever of Jacky to answer like that. It was all true, too. The B.B. looked at her with admiration.

"Durdlecombe must be a good place for shopping." The stranger again looked at the bulging bags with amusement and Jacky's manner became frigid. She had had enough of this stranger and she could imagine Mrs. Bly's disapproval if she could see them all at that moment. So frowning at the B.B. who were looking too friendly, she said.

"Thank you for warning us," and went on down the lane followed by her companions.

"Jacky . . . why did you suddenly snub him?"

"He was taking liberties . . . all very well to direct us, but it is no business of his what we have been doing. *Do* come on. I'm getting sick of being in the secret service."

It was rather a shock when they reached the shore and found the dumb fisherman singing "Onward Christian Soldiers" as he went on with his tarring, but he became dumb again as soon as he saw them and they decided Bill must be informed about it. He rowed them back to *La Belle Dame* and very lovely she looked as she lay becalmed on the sunlit sea; but there was no sign of her Skipper. They found him asleep in the cabin and awakened him with haste for the dumb singer of hymns was plainly waiting for his largesse.

"Hullo! So you have got back safely—all serene?"

"Absolutely, except that a spy questioned us on our way back," said Georgie.

A peculiar look came over Bill's face which puzzled

Jacky; surely, he had not gone to the trouble of arranging a meeting with a stranger because he wanted to make more excitement for the B.B.?

"What sort of a spy?"

"Oh, I don't know . . . a naval man. Jacky got rid of him and said we had been to fetch ship's stores from Durdlecombe."

"Good for Jack . . . he's plainly cut out for the S.S."

"That dumb man is waiting for his fare," Bert looked through the port-hole. "You said he was dumb, but he can jolly well sing."

Bill departed hastily, paid off the man, and when he returned asked, "Well—enjoy your tea?"

"Scrumptious! Thank you for treating us. Mr. Lillywhite has sent you some farm butter and things."

"Good of him . . . but I shan't be on board for a few days so you can take 'em as a present to the Chief of your tribe—now, how would you like to have a look at Lulworth Cove?"

"Gorgeous! But you know we have to be back by eight o'clock."

A slight breeze made sailing exhilarating and Bill set himself out to make the rest of the day pleasant. He allowed the crew to help sail the yacht, steer her, and in every way tried to give them a good time. They passed the gap at Lulworth Cove, a fairy cup enclosed by green cliffs, and they saw the sunny glen of White Horse. Then, they had to turn homewards and had a picnic supper on deck, hot cocoa and some of Mrs. Lillywhite's scones thickly spread with butter.

"Will you ever ask us again?" enquired Georgie. "We would *love* to come—wouldn't we, chaps?"

Every member of the B.B. including its leader

answered with complete enthusiasm and Bill seemed pleased.

"Well, you've shaped very well as an emergency crew and I shall be pleased to employ you again if ever I need help. Oh, I say . . . the whole family has come to meet you!"

It was quite true that the whole school, including the staff and Christopher Columbus had come down to the shore to meet the travellers and the Professor, wearing his Indian Chief's hat with his cricketing clothes was in deep conversation with Sam Jeans who certainly did not suffer from dumbness.

"Oh, dear . . . I do hope we are not late." Jacky was always afraid she would break school rules and be considered a nuisance.

"Of course we are not . . . two minutes early, in fact. I had better row over with you and give my salaams."

When Mrs. Bly saw her radiant pupils simply bursting with good health and good spirits after their day's outing she decided she had done well in allowing them to go. She was particularly anxious that Roberta should settle down as she had never been happy in any school and her parents had hopes of Rainbow End. Jacky too, looked less anxious and it looked as if she was having a good influence over her three most difficult girls in spite of her own strange upbringing.

Therefore, when Bill rowed over to deliver his charges and Felicity cried, "Oh, Mr. Bill, do you think you *will* invite me on your ship?" he immediately gave her an invitation which, to everyone's surprise Mrs. Bly accepted with gratitude.

CHAPTER IX

VILLAGE CRICKET

THE voyagers said nothing of their visit to The Jolly Mariners as Bill had impressed them so solemnly about keeping silent though he had extorted no promises. Jacky didn't care for mysteries; but she saw no harm in keeping silent on this point and allow Bill and the B.B. to have their harmless fun. Fortunately, too, they were not questioned too closely about the day's doings because their school friends had some exciting news of their own to impart. It seemed that morning hand-bills had been delivered by the baker's boy at Rainbow End and one of these was thrust under the noses of the home-comers as soon as Bill had departed:

Oyez!   Oyez!   Oyez!
All good people take notice
That on
August 3rd Next
A Grand Match of Cricket
Will Take Place On
The Village Green, Broomy Hill, Dorset
Between
The Broomy Hill XI
and
Two Players
Of Surrey and Kent
In this match history will be repeated, being in

*Truth a Test in Cricket the same that took place
One Hundred Years ago at Broomy Hill, the Two
Players on that occasion proving triumphant!,
Wickets pitched at 12.30 p.m.
On the same day a Great Fayre will be held on the
Village Green at which Fun and Jollity will go
hand-in-hand.*
God Save the Queen

"Then that decides it!" cried Roberta, no longer
"Bert" of the B.B. but a Broomy Hill cricketing fan.
"I shan't go home for the hols . . . at least not until
after August 3rd."

"Go home for the hols!" Jacky looked bewildered,
then went cold with dismay. *Surely* the camp wouldn't
break up like ordinary schools at the end of July. She
had understood they were all to stay there till the end
of September.

"Yes," went on Roberta, "didn't you know? You
can stay here, of course, but the parents want me to go
to Wales with them."

"And are you going, too?" Jacky asked Georgie
and Jerry.

"No, we are here for the whole time. Won't it be
fun when we've got all day free with no work to do?"

"I don't know—anyway, I can't see Bee living with
anyone with nothing to do." Jacky turned into the
tent feeling suddenly homeless again and wondering if
she should talk to Mrs. Bly about it.

She summoned up courage to do this next morning
and approached the headmistress with something of her
old defiance.

"Oh, please—will you tell me if I ought to write to

Dick or the Vicarage or someone about going away for the holidays?"

The Professor and Mrs. Bly had already talked this over and had no wish to lose this rather strange child, Jacintha Drew, described by the Professor as the "most sensible girl in the school" and more suited to be head girl than Cecilia.

"My dear child . . . do you want to leave Rainbow End?"

"Rather not." Jacky swallowed hard. "I love it."

"Well, we love having you. Some of the girls here join their parents which I think is a pity, breaking up the party before the end of the summer. You are very helpful Jacintha, dear, and the Professor and I always feel happy when you are with the girls, especially Felicity, who, as you see, is a little undisciplined because she has been so delicate and such a worry to us."

At this unexpected praise Jacky glowed with pleasure and burned to serve these kind people in some way for trusting her and making her one of them. Then she blushed hotly for she suddenly had a dreadful feeling that she ought not to have landed with the pupils on a strange coast and visited The Jolly Mariners.

"And you can help me more and more," continued Mrs. Bly, who knew more about Jacky's character than the girl guessed and was anxious to put her mind at rest.

"Oh, Mrs. Bly . . . how please? I'll do anything! Has Mrs. Jeans given notice?"

"No, thank goodness, nor has Doris, and that's a good deal due to you, too, dear. You made Mrs. Jeans welcome and now, like Doris, she seems one of the family. What I mean is you can help me in the holidays with Felicity and Ethel . . . you know how tiresome

Ethel can be and they are both inclined to get out of hand. Ethel has a certain 'pertness' which is most unattractive. I should be glad if you could interest them and hold out a guiding hand sometimes. Cecilia and Audrey's methods to the two smallest girls of the school is far too snubbing; it makes them indignant."

"I'll try, really and truly I will, Mrs. Bly. Felicity is a darling, but I can't pretend I'm fond of Ethel." Jacky gave a grin and Mrs. Bly smiled as she walked away for she could see Jacky was happier and no longer felt unwanted.

Because the Broomy Hill XI was going to take part in a cricket match, Rainbow End cricketers seemed to think it was their duty to distinguish themselves, too, and play became constant in their recreation hours and enthusiasm for the game increased by leaps and bounds. One night Bill Briggs turned up to watch the play and said he considered Georgie almost as good as any member of the village team; that Jacky, as a fast bowler showed herself supple and cunning of hand and that Miss Carroll's "pace" was magnificent. Such praise was stimulating and when Bill kept his promise and persuaded the village team to come over one Saturday afternoon and give them a match, the beating they got was almost a triumph, for the Broomy Hill captain congratulated them heartily on their play.

If Mrs. Bly's dreams of her pupils gracefully performing Greek dances on the sands were disappointing she said nothing for there was no doubt that all the girls were happy, interested, and content. Lessons were not neglected by anyone except the cricket-mad Professor and nobody had any time on their hands for Satan to play with and even Ethel—praised by Bill for a good

" catch "—seemed to forget she was the school critic.

Before leaving, the captain of the village team made a request to his host and hostess. He explained to them that the Great Fayre to be held on the same day as the cricket match was in aid of the local hospital and if any kind people at Rainbow End could help them to raise funds by stalls, or some sort of entertainment the village would be extremely grateful.

" Of course we will," promised Mrs. Bly. " Girls do you hear that? We are to sit down and make tea cosies and things for a stall."

This remark caused so little enthusiasm that she said, " What an uncharitable family we are . . . nobody wants to work, so can anyone suggest something else?"

" They want entertainment," suggested Miss Carroll. " Why not give them an exhibition of folk-dancing on the Green and make a collection for the hospital?"

" That's a *splendid* idea!" Mrs. Bly felt her dreams were coming true at last. Then Cecilia had another idea. " Why not get the village infants down here after school and teach them to dance ' Hey Boys!' We should then be doing them a good turn as well as the hospital."

" I think everyone would much rather pay to watch them dance than *us* . . . especially their mothers and fathers," said Georgie, who had never been keen on folk-dancing and the Professor said this was very sound psychology.

" And couldn't we take one of the wigwams and get it up as a stall and sell Indian souvenirs, beads and bows and arrows. I know how to make them," added Jacky.

This suggestion was an immense success and voices

clamoured to offer themselves as saleswomen in the wigwam and Felicity at once extracted a promise from the Professor to buy her a squaw's dress.

"But how on earth we are going to do all this in a month—goodness knows," groaned Georgie. "Cricket practice, lessons, bathing, making bows and arrows, teaching village brats dances."

"A good thing we have no S.S. duties," whispered Bert.

"Surely Bill will invite us again soon," answered Jerry, and Georgie frowning at them both went on to say, "I really don't know how things will get done and after all our dreams of basking in the sun with nothing to do, too!"

Cricket began really in earnest and though Bill Briggs said no more about cruising he came over several times to do some coaching because privately he thought the Professor's play was too classical.

Bill had "dash" and was a faster bowler than the Professor, altogether a more spectacular player which appealed to the young.

"Bowl from the hips!" he would yell, and here Miss Carroll's teaching came in useful and soon a correct and effective body swing was the team's greatest asset. Bill could make a ball break very quickly; a method which Jacky, especially, copied with great success. "Go on practising," were always his parting words. "If you are done up after sending a few overs it shows you are a weakling . . . a good bowler wants an hour a day at it to get his arm loose."

"But Mr. Briggs . . . they are not going to play for the county," remonstrated Mrs. Bly thinking things were getting just a little *too* professional, and Bill answered, "Oh well . . . you never know," and he looked at his watch and said he must fly as he had lent *La Belle Dame* to a friend and was expecting her back that night and would go to meet her.

"Could we go too?" entreated the B.B.

"Rather not . . . goodness knows when she will arrive in. Professor could you lend me that fat donkey and the cart? I want to land some old gear and I can't get the car on to the foreshore."

"My dear fellow . . . the donkey and the cart belong to Jacintha there."

"Really?" Bill looked perplexed and said, "Well, Jack, what about lending them to me for one night?"

"Of course, but please promise not to overload Slowboy and we always give him some oats after he's been working."

"I'll treat him like a king and feast him on oats and all and return him to-morrow with all my gratitude. By the way, I am having a sort of birthday next Satur- day and *La Belle Dame* will be receiving guests from 12.30 to 4, and all are welcome. I've chartered the *Seabird* and Sam for the day to row you over."

"Do you mean we are *all* invited?"

"A hearty welcome is extended to all. Miss Cecilia . . . we shall be at anchor, so you need have no fears."

Cecilia was a bad sailor and vowed she would never board the yacht.

Bill went off in the donkey-cart pulled by Slowboy and the B.B. watched them curiously.

"What do you suppose he wants them for?"

"Goodness knows!" Jacky seemed a little gloomy. "I hope old Slowboy isn't going to be dragged into any spy work . . . he has always been so respectable."

Sam brought the donkey back the following day as slow and sleek as ever and in the cart was a large parcel addressed to Jacky.

"Surely Bill isn't getting reckless and sending despatches to the school?" said Georgie. "Open it, Jack."

Jacky did so eagerly for though nobody knew it but herself this was the first parcel she had ever received and she felt excited. It contained a magnificent box of chocolates tied with a gigantic bow of sea-blue ribbon and the words: *Many thanks for Slowboy and the chariot. I gave the moke a grand tuck-in of oats and all and hope his mistress will graciously accept a box of Cadbury's Best . . . Bill.*

"How frightfully nice of him! There's one thing I must say about the S.S. it does feed you jolly well," said Georgie

The whole school feasted on Cadbury's Best and Jacky felt enormously happy having something to share after sharing many feasts with her friends and she was grateful to Bill.

Saturday turned out to be a gorgeous summer day and they could see *La Belle Dame* decorated with a gay little row of streamers.

The first visiting party skimming over the calm sea in the *Seabird* and found Bill and Steve in gala dress; the decks spick and span and refreshments consisting of many kinds of sandwiches, cakes, biscuits, coffee, tea, lemonade and ice-cream awaiting them in the cabin. The B.B. having once acted as temporary crew on a cruise were more at home on the yacht than the rest and were called upon to act as hostesses which seemed to annoy Ethel Forbes. She and Georgie would have had words about it if Jacky, remembering her promise to Mrs. Bly, had not distracted Ethel's attention by asking her and Felicity to come into the ship's galley and help her make more coffee.

Doris, of course, was present and her appearance was sensational. She had spent the preceding afternoon in the village and in anticipation of visiting a yacht for the first time had bought herself a nautical costume consisting of a very jaunty little nautical hat and a reefer coat with brass buttons.

She shrieked loudly when ascending and descending the ladder and was delighted to accept a coloured photograph of *La Belle Dame* as a souvenir when she left. The Skipper was extremely generous. The girls were all presented with sweets, the ladies with flowers and the Professor was overwhelmed by a gift of cigars.

" But my dear Briggs . . . you are too generous. I only smoke a cigar as the greatest treat."

" Well, keep 'em as a treat . . . or smoke 'em instead of the Peace Pipe in your Wigwam." The box was pushed into the Professor's hands and the guests, well-nourished and well-entertained left the hospitable yacht quite in love with Mr. Bill Briggs and entirely forgetting they had once believed him to be a kidnapper or a murderer.

The teachers of the village school were next approached and the offer made to teach the pupils folk-dancing and it was received in the usual simple village way everyone concerned saying amiably, " they didn't mind if they did." Times were fixed for the visits and soon the green slopes round Rainbow End looked like a scene from Merrie England when the first Elizabeth was on the throne and village lads and lassies came out to play in great strength.

Meanwhile preparations went on in aid of the Fair, which was to be spread round the Village Green in the old style with booths and stalls. Jacky made the B.B. tramp miles in search of willow wands and birch bark which were brought back and lessons in basket-weaving in the Indian way were given daily to anyone interested. She made bows and arrows, too, and necklaces of dried orange and lemon pips dyed orange and scarlet. The Professor was to lend his best fossils—for exhibition only—but only half promised to lecture on them in case he could not bear to be away from the cricket match.

Mrs. Bly and Miss Lyle promised to judge at the Baby Show, Miss Carroll would, of course, have her hands full with the folk-dancing. Doris, was going to carry round the cake made by Mrs. Jeans for a cake-weighing competition.

Because Felicity had a squaw dress Ethel's kind Mamma sent one to her, too, and they were both told they could sell necklaces and bows and arrows out-side the wigwam.

Cecilia and Audrey decided to dress up as gipsies and sell charms and the four-leaved clovers they had discovered in a meadow.

Several of the girls who had planned to go home at the end of the term begged to stay a little longer not wishing to miss any of the excitement.

Then, when everything, including the weather, seemed to be set fair, a bombshell descended on the Broomy Hill Cricket XI.

CHAPTER X

COME TO THE FAIR!

IT was the baker's boy who brought the news. He was a grandson of Farmer Farley and a promising member of the Broomy Hill XI; and his ambition was to become a professional cricketer and play for England. The coming match meant so much to him and his mind was so full of scores and runs and victories that he very often left the wrong loaves for his customers which made Mrs. Jeans vow that his head would be more useful as a cricket-ball. He arrived one morning exactly a fortnight before the match and announced that his captain had received the news that the " Two Players " were unable to fulfil their promise to play.

" A dirty trick if ever there was one," he said to his astonished audience all summoned to hear the dire news. " Bills out and all. I've stuck 'em on all the trees for a mile myself and there's a bus running from Dorchester on purpose to see the play. My grandad says they've got wind we're going to win and won't face it."

"What a nice, cricketing spirit," remarked Miss Lyle and the Professor added, "Well, my lad . . . *you've* all got to face it and get another team to play against you. Remember *Audaces fortuna juvat.*"

" Yes, sir," said Joe, who having never learned Latin remembered nothing of the sort.

" You'll have to have lots more bills printed with

Cancelled written across them," said Ethel rather unsympathetically, "and Felicity and I will distribute them." Both Ethel and Felicity were curious and loved to see other people's houses.

Joe had no sooner departed than Mr. Bill Briggs came up the steps from the beach having spent the night on *La Belle Dame* and had heard the bad news from Sam Jeans.

"There's only one thing for it," he said. "You'll have to tackle it, and after all, why not? The team can face fast bowling like all good batsmen and the captain of the Broomy Hill team is a corker . . . and can send down a slow one, too, with the best."

"My *dear* chap! These girls are all good, but I don't suppose the villagers would deign to play with schoolgirls."

"*Wouldn't* they? As a matter of fact the captain is coming along the moment he's finished his milk-round to ask you."

Bill did not add that this was by his suggestion, and added: "Now is the time to show yourselves good sports and ready to take on anything. Didn't some great man say once, 'Good cricketers make the best ambassadors in the world'?"

The Professor was flattered, alarmed, and anxious to be a sport so when the captain of the village team arrived he was ready to listen to any suggestions. It seemed that the match had been well advertised and it was likely to attract many visitors staying round the coast. Some explanation of the change of plans would have to be given, of course, and he suggested "a bit should be put in the local paper." Fortunately, there was to be no gate-money so nobody could ask for their money back: all money received from other attractions on the Fair-ground would go to the Fund.

The Professor—after consulting his excited team—consented and when Mrs. Bly heard the captain say that "all this here dancing had given the girls such good footwork in the field that it was a treat to watch 'em," she murmured in a pleased way, "He means rhythm, grace and balance."

Then Mr. Bill Briggs had another idea. He suggested that he and the Professor should appear as the "Two Players" of a hundred years ago when most cricketers wore those odd hats half-bowler and half-topper and were usually, too, heavily bearded like the late cricket star W. G. Grace, the greatest batsman of his time. Bill said he was certain the Broomy Hill team had some of these old hats and the beards could be false.

The Professor said he already had a beard and had no objection at all to looking like a Player of a hundred years ago; in fact, as usual he was made happy by the idea of dressing-up.

"Your beard, Professor, though elegant, I grant you, is of the wrong Elizabethan period. It must not be small and pointed, but black and bushy like W. G.'s. You must wear a false one and so shall I, and if our batting and bowling and fielding take after our beards we shall get the crowd's attention and nobody will think of asking for his money back."

The Professor insisted upon handing over the captaincy to Bill who was pleased to accept it and he promised to be over as often as possible to train them to be a fit side for the Broomy Hill XI.

He kept his promise with a vengeance and worked

them all to the point of exhaustion and at the same time created a keenness which surprised him.

Unfortunately being "Players" prevented four of the girls, the B.B., from being stall-holders; but Cecilia and Audrey were not in the team so could remain gipsies and there were other girls not returning home till after the match to help at the Fair, too. Some of these volunteered to carry tea-trays from the tea-tent to people watching the cricket.

To Ethel's great delight Jacky suggested that she and Felicity should take charge of the wigwam as neither the Professor nor the B.B. could now undertake it.

The weather continued glorious and on the morning of the great day there was that hazy blue mist called by country people "the pride of the morning" which always means a fine, hot day.

Everyone was up at a very early hour for there was much to do and the wigwam had to be taken down and conveyed to the village green in the donkey-cart. Mrs. Jeans—who had also promised to help with "Teas"—arrived in a flowery overall instead of her usual man's cap and tweed skirt and apron.

The B.B. loaded the wigwam and all the things made for sale into the cart. There were also some of the Professor's fossils which he had labelled and described for the visitors.

When they reached the green, people were already busy there and it was all very gay and truly in "the goode old style" of a country Fair. The stalls surrounded the green and the old cricket-pitch had been watered and rolled so thoroughly that it was a vivid green. Chairs and trestle tables were being brought from the Village Hall to the tea tent and the Vicar's two sons were putting up a coconut shy and an Aunt Sally.

They pitched the tent and hung the fossils round the walls and placed the baskets, bows and arrows, etc. outside the door to attract customers.

"It looks *lovely*," said Felicity, who had now arrived with Ethel both attired in the Red Indian squaw dresses. "And remember I'm the head squaw and you are to ask *me* anything asked about the fossils," announced Ethel who was considered learned in fossil-lore.

"Then if you are the head squaw and so important you had better think of some way of filling up the tent, it looks much too empty," said Georgie.

"There aren't enough fossils. I always said we ought to have found another *Ichthyosaurus Platydon*," added Jerry.

"I was just thinking the same thing and I've got an idea." Jacky looked excited. "What about my Japanese prints? We could put them all round and pin a notice outside: *Exhibition of Japanese Art*."

"But where are they?"

"The Professor has them . . . but of course he'll let me have them. I say, Cecilia could I borrow Queen and run home for something I want?" Cecilia and Audrey came up leading their ponies that were to be lent for children's rides.

"Of course, but don't let her get too hot, she'll have a pretty strenuous afternoon, I suppose."

"Thanks awfully." Jacky rode away and was soon back with her old portfolio containing the prints and these were arranged all round the tent to everyone's intense satisfaction.

There was not much time after that for stumps were to be struck at twelve-thirty; in fact people were arriving on bicycles and cars in order to make a day of it on the pleasant green, and picnic parties were already encamped ready to enjoy a good game of cricket on a real summer day. As the girls left to rush home for a hasty lunch a bus came up and deposited a crowd of holiday-makers outside the Village Hall, and with the knowledge that all these people had come to watch them play, the members of the Rainbow End XI began to suffer from acute stage-fright.

They wore cool frocks and caps with peaks to protect them from the blazing sun and when the Professor and Bill emerged from the dressing-tent there was loud laughter for they wore false beards and the hats of a hundred years ago which looked extremely funny.

"My dears," said the Professor, " I must obey our captain and it's all for a good cause but if W. G. endured what I am enduring in *his* beard on a day like this, and still remained 'the batsman of all batsmen,' he must indeed have been a genius."

" And all remember I want genius in the field as well as at the wicket," cautioned Bill. " George, old chap, it's up to you."

When the Rainbow End XI marched on to the green there were crowds of spectators all seated on the grass and they were received with cheers, especially the bearded Two Players. Many of the people had not seen the bit in the local paper, and thought they were professional players in a very odd and amusing cricketing mood.

Play began promptly and the Broomy Hill team, having won the toss, went in for first innings and sent in their best batsman who made a fine showing. The score rose freely, fifty going up in thirty minutes, before the batsman was bowled by Bill Briggs.

But as the score of their rivals rose the spirits of the Rainbow End team flagged, especially Jacky's who for some unknown reason always felt it was her fault if things went wrong for the school. "We're going to get a beating," she thought. "Well, I expected that, but I do wish we could make a better show." Then suddenly the tables turned. The batsman had taken guard and glancing at the field he saw Georgie was standing very deep at cover point. He accordingly placed a ball in that direction thinking this was a chance for an easy run. But as he *played* the ball, Georgie, remembering all Bill's orders about good fielding showed a wonderful quickness of brain and movement and stole in a yard or two to the right and caught the ball a few inches from the ground, a really brilliant catch. This was greeted with great applause and cries of "Well caught!" "Well caught!" which was music to the ears of the Rainbow End XI.

From that moment luck descended on their team and deserted Broomy Hill, for, as somebody says in *Tom Brown's Schooldays*, "*The goddess who presides over cricket loves to bring ill-luck to the most skilful players*," and the match ended with victory for Rainbow End by 20 runs.

The weather had played a great part in making it a success, for everyone was in holiday mood and the ten helpers had shown great enterprise by bringing trays of tea to the spectators. Cecilia, too, had done well

with her four leaved clovers and charms and Ethel and
Felicity had done a roaring trade in bows and arrows,
but not so much in necklaces. Ethel had lectured on
the fossils in the manner of the Professor and had never
enjoyed herself so much.

But when the B.B.—now famous cricketers—rushed
in to see how things were and with hopes that Ethel
and Felicity would go and fetch them much-needed tea
all they found were two exhausted squaws and two
empty ice-cream cartons.

" What little pigs you are. You might have got something ready for us!"

"Well, I like that . . . we haven't had a second.
Cecilia brought us the ices. I say, girls, there's been
such a funny man here and ordered us not to leave the
tent without anyone in it."

" Whatever for?"

" He kept looking at Jacky's pictures and he got
terribly excited and kept on saying, 'Upon my soul!
It's incredible!' and things like that. He asked us who
owned the pictures and we told him Jacky and he said,
' Tell the young lady I will be greatful if she will see me
when the match ends!' . . . He's coming now!"

A tall, thin man most unlike the rest of the merry-
makers on the village green was approaching the wigwam talking very solemnly to the Professor—who had
removed his beard—and Mrs. Bly.

As they entered the tent Mrs. Bly said, " This is
Jacintha Drew—and Jacky this is Mr. Foster from
London. He is an artist and is very much interested in
your prints . . . it seems they are valuable."

" That's what the other artist said—the one who took

our cottage. He said he wished he could afford to buy them.''

"Well Mr. Foster wants to buy them now . . . he feels quite horrified to see them lying about like this.''

"But before Jacky makes up her mind,'' said the Professor, "she must of course consult her step-father.''

"Oh no, please, Professor . . . I needn't, they are *mine* . . . in any case Dick would say sell them if I can.''

"How did they come in your possession, Miss Jacintha?'' asked the visitor.

"My mother left them to me. Her father, my grand-father, was in Japan for years and he brought them home with him. I do like them awfully, but I don't know much about them.''

"I can see that. If you did you wouldn't have exhibited them in all the wrong sequence. The series represents a pilgrimage to Fujiyama, the sacred Japanese mountain, and each picture shows the pilgrims getting nearer and nearer to the summit. They are lovely and very old prints and must have some time belonged to some noble Japanese family . . . may I put them in order?''

"Oh, please do.'' They all gathered round and the artist arranged the pictures with Fujiyama getting nearer and nearer. Everybody expressed their admira-tion and Jacky suddenly felt a lump in her throat. Not only were these pictures beautiful, but they were her very own, and the only things she possessed in the world. Perhaps some day she would realise her dearest wish and have a home of her own with a wall on which to hang the pictures.

"Don't you want to sell them, Jacky?" asked the Professor kindly.

Jacky hesitated and then, remembering she had no money except what she called her "egg money," as Mrs. Bly would insist upon paying for the eggs laid by the hens, she said, "I would rather give them to you and Mrs. Bly please because . . . because"—she went scarlet—"I owe you such a lot, you know."

The Professor and Mrs. Bly exchanged looks and Mrs. Bly said, "Oh *no*, Jacky. We couldn't accept anything so valuable—but will keep them for you, in trust you know and if ever you do want to sell them perhaps Mr. Foster will help us."

Mr. Foster, who was staying in the neighbourhood and had seen the cricket-match advertised and thought it might be interesting, had arrived to find it was just a match between the village team and schoolgirls, and a little indignant had wandered round the Fair ground and discovered the tent where two little girls had wanted him to buy fossils and bead necklaces. He was greatly disappointed he could not buy the rare old prints he discovered there, and leaving his card he departed after saying that if they changed their minds he would be delighted to make a good offer.

The Rainbow End XI then went to the tent to have tea with their rivals and Joe Farley remarked that he did not intend to wait another hundred years before giving the Two Players "a licking." They cheered each other loudly and were content because the Fair had been an immense success and the village money bags were full.

When three of the members of the B.B. settled in their tent that night burnt black with the sun and with blistered hands and aching limbs but gloriously happy, Georgie said, "I bet if Jacky had never come here and made us all mad on cricket and invented the B.B. we should have just gone on what Audrey calls 'posturing' on the sands and would never have had any fun at all."

"And if Jacky hadn't made us mad on cricket Mr. Foster would never have gone into the wigwam and seen the pictures," added Jerry, "and now Jacky can be *rich* if she likes to sell them . . . lucky girl!"

"*Rich!*" Jacky could hardly believe her ears. Here were these two girls she had so much envied calling *her*, the homeless Jacky, rich and lucky, and to think it was really true and she had had to come to Rainbow End to find she owned a treasure.

CHAPTER XI

THE SCHOONER "HESPERUS"

AFTER the excitement of the cricket match things seemed a little slow and they heard nothing from Mr. Bill Briggs for nearly a week.

Then, Mr. Jeans arrived with a note from him for Mrs. Bly asking if Jacky, Georgie, Jerry, Bert and Felicity might go sailing with him the following Saturday.

Felicity, of course, was enraptured, but the B.B. felt a little piqued.

"Bill must have gone batty to invite that kid," said Georgie.

"Well, I hope he understands he has to be careful

what he does and says or she'll come back and prattle about it."

"I suppose it's because he promised her, and *you* needn't grouse about it, Georgie—*I* shall be the one made responsible for her and watch she doesn't go overboard." Jacky sighed.

As a matter of fact this is exactly what Felicity's anxious mother did and Felicity was told she could go only on the condition that she obeyed Jacky. Ethel was broken-hearted and wailed so continually that "it wasn't fair" that Felicity became miserable, too, and begged her mother to write and ask if Ethel might be included in the invitation.

"Certainly not. Ethel must learn to bear disappointments and Father will take her fossil-hunting instead."

Even the B.B.—never overfond of Ethel—thought this a poor substitute for a cruise on the Lovely Lady and they generously gave Ethel the freedom of Neptune's wigwam during their absence which made her forgive them for going but to hate Bill Briggs for slighting her though in reality he had not realised that there was any such person as Ethel Forbes.

Saturday, dawned like most days in that wonderful summer hot and sunny, and when the party boarded the yacht Jacky immediately sought out Bill.

"Well, captain . . . why so glum?"

"I'm worried . . . promise me you won't send us to strange places this time because nothing would induce me to take Felicity, or to leave her here alone with you . . . in case you *are* a murderer! Besides, I don't think the B.B. would go anywhere without me and, as no doubt you have discovered they are not as able to deal with dangerous situations as I am after my life in the wilds."

"That's all right, captain . . . don't worry. I'm the one who's going to do the dirty work ashore this time and you are all to stay aboard and keep house."

"Oh Bill . . . is it safe? I don't mind myself, but I should hate to be lost at sea or anything like that with Felicity on my hands. She is a ewe lamb, you know."

At that moment "the crew," who had been enjoying themselves swabbing decks and helping themselves to the chocolate biscuits set out in the cabin, arrived upon the scene and asked Bill about his plans for the day.

"I'm going to meet a pal in the channel, he'll be in the schooner *Hesperus*. No, don't look incredulous, he really does sail the *Hesperus* and he's a Frenchman and a nice chap. She's a bigger boat than my Lovely Lady and I thought while we have our chat you might like to board her and see her insides. That O.K. captain?" Bill looked at Jacky inquiringly.

"It *sounds* jolly."

"Sounds jolly! I should think it does!" The B.B. were in transports of delight and Felicity said, "Oh Jacky *please* don't look like the parents do when they are going to say we can't do nice things! It will be marvellous to visit the *Hesperus*."

"Hope you all speak French?"

"Jacky can . . . though Miss Lyle says her accent is abominable."

"The captain certainly seems a Jack of all trades. Now my lads, come along and help me set the mainsail while George takes the helm for a spot."

Before they had kept close to the coast and sailed

westwards; but on this occasion they headed eastwards leaving the bold, but friendly crags and cliffs that made a continuous, ever-changing panorama behind them and heading for the open sea. The weather conditions were halcyon and the yacht skimmed over a peaceful sea. To see the miles of blue, heaving sea ahead of them was exciting and for the first time the crew really enjoyed the pleasures of sailing. Jacky, once more the cook, took Felicity with her to the galley where she kept her under her own eye and instructed her in the making of a spotted Dick. She set her to watch over it on the galley stove while she went aft to talk to the Skipper.

"I say, Bill, how far are we now from France?"

"A long way; but if this breeze freshens we shall begin to skip along nicely . . . do you want to call on our neighbours and show off your 'abominable' French accent?"

"I'd love to go to France . . . but don't be *too* reckless, will you? It seems risky to me to be out on the open sea like this with only one person on board who can really sail a ship. When I think of what might happen if you *did* fall overboard I go quite cold with terror."

"We'll be all right. You mustn't panic, captain, it brings ill-luck to the ship."

"But what would happen if a sudden squall came up . . . the sort of thing that always happens in a book?"

"Nothing. My 'Lovely Lady' is a clever little woman and knows what she is doing. Can't you *feel* how she is enjoying making good and cutting a nice clean way through the water?"

"Sail-O!" shouted Georgie, who with the rest of the

crew was perched on the cabin roof thoroughly enjoying their voyage and taking turns to look through the Skipper's glasses. "Do you think it's the schooner *Hesperus* sailing the summer sea?"

"Let's have a look," Bill took the glasses. "Yes, that's the *Hesperus* . . . lovely thing, isn't she?"

The crew crowded forward to watch the lovely line of the approaching schooner; her spread sails skimming over the water like white wings.

"How shall we board her?"

"She'll heave to and send a dinghy to fetch you along. You'll visit the *Hesperus* while her Skipper and I have our pow-wow and you can carry on the *entente cordiale*, too, for the Skipper, like the one in the poem has brought his little daughter, 'to bear him company'."

"Oh Bill . . . has he really and will she be French?"

"Children of French parents usually *are* French, I believe. That's why I invited Felicity . . . they must be about the same age."

"But I can't speak French." Felicity, who, hearing the excitement had left the spotted Dick to its fate, began to wail.

"Well, now you see the advantages of foreign travel and when you go home again you'll be all for learning languages. Do you see that? They are putting out the dinghy."

A man in a blue jersey with "Hesperus" across it had put out from the schooner and was rowing towards the yacht and the girls watched its approach with excitement.

"Bill, aren't you coming too?" Jacky still felt

uncertain about the excursion though she was just as anxious to visit the French boat as the others.

"I'll come and fetch you in an hour. Hullo, Jacques!"

The sailor, dark-eyed and swarthy, grinned as he brought the dinghy alongside and cried, "*Bonjour, monsieur, Bonjour mesdemoiselles!*"

"I think we ought to take our coats," said Jacky in what Felicity called her "parent" manner and this suggestion was greeted with indignation.

"Why . . . it's boiling hot!"

"Really Jacky . . . you talk like a great-grand-mother!"

"The French kid will laugh at us."

"I don't care it's safer, don't you think so, Skipper?"

"You are the boss . . . why not take macintoshes, too, and a couple of umbrellas?"

But Jacky was adamant and refused to go until everyone had fetched a cardigan and at last the ladder was let down for them to descend into the dinghy and each "mademoiselle" was received in a firm grip by Jacques and overwhelmed by the smell of garlic.

"*Au revoir!*" Bill waved his hand and there they were all rocking on the waves on their way to the *Hesperus*. She was much larger and handsomer than *La Belle Dame* but without the latter's daintiness and her paint was decidedly dingy and she had a slightly neglected look as if she suffered from an inefficient crew. A little man, evidently the owner, hung on the bulwarks watching their approach and standing by him was the oddest little girl. A little older than Felicity, she wore her hair in long sausage curls nearly down to her waist, and tied in a large blue bow of ribbon at the top of her head and her frock was of wool tartan piped with a hideous bright green, a most unsuitable garment for a hot afternoon on the ocean. She seemed to be in a state of excitement and waved her hands continuously and shouted "*Bonjour mesdemoiselles!*" over and over again.

"Thank goodness '*Bonjour*' seems to be the only word they know of their own language," remarked Georgie. "Even I can manage that—come on girls we must wave back and shriek or they will think we don't want to visit them."

She immediately stood up and began to wave and call "*Bonjour! Bonjour!*" in an exaggerated French way and the others, not to be out done followed her example.

The dead calm made boarding the schooner an easy matter but Jacky was thankful to get Felicity safely on deck and released the firm grip she had on her skirt while the whole party exchanged bows and greetings with their hosts.

To the consternation of the B.B. the Skipper and his little daughter poured out a torrent of French which was answered by the amazing Jacky. True, Jacky's French did not sound exactly like the others, but at least they understood it and her friends and admirers were especially charmed by the way she used her hand and shrugged her shoulders with real French elegance.

"*Vos amies . . . elles ne parlent pas francais, n'est-ce-pas?*" enquired the Skipper, and Jacky replied mischievously:

"*Vraiment . . . c'est le mot ' Bonjour'.*"

At this the little girl laughed heartily and the B.B.

annoyed racked their brains to remember some French
suitable for a visit to a schooner.

"*La! La!*" said the Skipper to the little girl. "*Est-
ce que vous ne parlez pas l'anglais et vous n'avez pas
des manières, mon enfant?*" and the little girl looked
daggers at the guests and said in slow, painful English:
"Will you please come to the cabin, my friends?"

"I'm not going to be able to stand this kid . . . she's
worse than Ethel," murmured Georgie but she managed
to smile sweetly and even murmured "*Merci bien,*"
which she hoped was the French equivalent of "Thanks
awfully," and Felicity, not caring for the way the
French child looked at her hastily recalled yesterday's
French lesson and waving her hand at the sea
remarked haughtily, "*La mer est bleu!*"

The Skipper seemed as anxious now to get his guests
down below as he had been pleased to welcome them
and he hurried them down the companion-way to the
state cabin and Annette, still chattering, led the way.
They would have much rather stayed on deck and
explored and seen the crew, but too polite to say so
they followed Annette's tartan skirt and bobbing
corkscrew curls below to the cabin.

It was totally unlike the cabin of "*La Belle Dame*"
and much larger and more luxurious but hideous in its
decorations. Lace curtains tied back with red bands
were draped over the port-holes; the mattresses on the
seats were of red plush and there was a mirror of tarn-
ished gilt. The centre table was covered with a red
cloth with bobbed fringe and instead of books on the
shelves there were many photographs, so like Annette
and her Papa, the Skipper, that there was no doubt they
belonged to a large family.

To their horror Annette invited them to sit down on the red plush seats and the Skipper waving his hand to them and entreating them to "be 'appy" disappeared and immediately Annette opened a cupboard and brought out a very large and elaborate box of chocolate creams and began to pass them round talking at a terrific rate while she did it.

"What on earth is she spouting about?" Georgie asked Jacky, who frowned at her while she tried to listen politely to Annette's rapid description of her life and the lives of all the relations in the photographs. Then, installing herself comfortably on the red plush and, seeming to find no discomfort from the hot cabin and her thick clothes, she filled her mouth with chocolate creams and invited her guests to relate their family histories.

Jacky gave her a brief description of Rainbow End, which she received with screams of surprise and delight and at once announced she would ask her Papa if she could attend this unusual school.

The B.B. began to fidget and Felicity nudged Jacky and said, "Do ask her if we can go on deck?"

Apparently Jacky put the question which was received with another torrent of French and many shrugs and hand waving.

"What on earth does she say?"

"She says she's fed up with being on deck." Jacky grinned.

"Well, I must say . . . do we have to sit in a row in this stuffy cabin till Bill fetches us." The B.B. were indignant and Felicity crept round to a port-hole but on looking out very disappointingly could see nothing but a heaving sea.

"Do be quiet—we just *have* to stick it—and all be thankful you don't have to make up conversation." Jacky was indignant, too.

The B.B. *were* thankful though they much regretted they had not been more industrious in their French studies for they really would have enjoyed asking Annette why she wore thick tartan on a hot summer day, and whether her mamma had never taught her it was impolite to put three chocolates in one's mouth at once.

They seemed to have been sitting in the hot cabin for hours when suddenly loud excited voices were heard on deck:

"*Mon Dieu! Quel malheur! Est-ce que le capitaine est tué?*"

Unable to control her curiosity, Annette rushed up the companion-way followed by her guests, Jacky, thinking in misery, "Oh dear . . . what has happened *now* . . . I felt in my bones we should never have left the yacht. Felicity, if you don't keep by me, I'll *hold your hand!* Can't you see the decks are all slippery?"

A sailor, the only one of the crew on board, was standing aft gazing at the yacht in the distance and the girls rushed to join him. The dinghy that had brought them to the *Hesperus* was now lying alongside *La Belle Dame* and the French Skipper and Jacques were on the deck of the yacht bending over somebody lying there.

Jacky's heart seemed to stand quite still; her premonition of coming disaster had proved true and Bill, their only friend and protector, was either dead or dying, and they were alone with foreigners out of England's sight.

"What is the matter, please?" She spoke to the man rapidly in French and he, with many gesticulations, told her.

"What does he say?" The girls pressed round Jacky.

"He says they had to load a small cargo on the yacht and Bill slipped on something—funny thing as Bill isn't clumsy—and he's hurt."

"*Tué*," cried Annette. "*Voyez, il ne bouge pas. Pauvre capitaine! Il est tué, sans doute!*"

"*Sans doute*," echoed the sailor ghoulishly and again the girls chorused, "What does he say?"

"Oh *do* be quiet. I'm sick of telling you what everyone says. I wish to goodness you'd had the brains to learn some French before we started!" Worried to death, Jacky forgot to be motherly and comforting.

"Well, you needn't get ratty. We can't all be clever and naturally we want to know what is happening."

Jerry was indignant, but Georgie, who never failed Jacky said, "Do be quiet . . . can't you see Jacky's got enough to do to listen to their lingo?"

Annette, who realised there was dispute in the air and realised that the girls did not understand said in her broken English solemnly, "Young ladies . . . your friend, the Captain, is now, I fear, dead."

The B.B. went pale and Felicity clung to Jacky and said, "Oh Jacky, it isn't true, is it?"

"I hope not . . . and I don't believe it is but for heaven's sake, Felicity, my duck, don't cry, but let these people see we can stand up to whatever happens." Jacky put her hand to her mouth and called "Captain Brun! Captain Brun!"

He came to the side of the boat and began to answer in French and Jacky's heart sank as she saw Bill's silent form.

"Mademoiselle, there has been a little mishap." (Oh, thank goodness, thought Jacky thankfully, surely he wouldn't call Bill's death " a little mishap ") " Your friend, Captain Briggs, has hit his head and is unconscious."

"Oh please, will you fetch us at once. I know how to bandage."

"No, no, that is not necessary, mademoiselle. All has been done by me with great skill, I assure you. We now carry him down to the cabin where he will rest."

It seemed unsympathetic to think of themselves at such a moment, but in her despair Jacky had to shout, "But what is to become of us?"

"Pardon, mademoiselle . . . but it is necessary for me to return to the patient . . . but I will return and discuss our plans."

He rushed back to Bill's recumbent form and the next thing the anxious watchers saw was it being lifted and carried down to the cabin.

"I suppose we daren't ask what he said," asked Jerry bitterly and Jacky answered tersely, "Yes, you may . . . he says poor Bill is hurt badly and for the moment he can't discuss *our* plans."

"Oh, poor old Bill . . . but I say, Jacky, what on earth are we going to do." Georgie was determined to be brave and share Jacky's awful responsibility.

"Keep our end up of course."

Annette began to chatter again; but when nobody took any notice she returned to the cabin and fetched what was left of the chocolate creams to console her friends, and was amazed when they refused them.

They stood anxiously watching the decks of *La Belle Dame* and it seemed ages before the men appeared again and then one remained and the Skipper of the *Hesperus* got into the dinghy and began to row towards the schooner.

Jacky ran to meet him. " Oh, please, Captain Brun. Is he much hurt?"

" It is a bad concussion, mademoiselle. That boy of his—a stupid fellow—left a rope badly coiled and it threw him, poor fellow."

" Will he get well?"

" But of course, mademoiselle . . . it is only a question of a few days and a few stiches in his head . . . in the meantime, mesdemoiselles, you are our guests."

CHAPTER XII

L'ENTENTE CORDIALE

When Jacky, aghast, had once more told her companions " what the Skipper had said " Georgie whistled in dismay, Bert shrugged her shoulders, and Jerry said, "Golly!" briefly, but Felicity, added to Jacky's despair by saying, " Mother will die of fits."

" I simply can't see why Bill can't have his head stitched up in England," said Georgie and Jerry interrupted by adding, "I say Jack . . . I don't want to look on the black side of things but do you think we are kidnapped?"

"Oh don't be silly for goodness' sake, I've got enough on my mind. I must say I've been in some jolly awkward corners in my time, but I've never been lost in the Channel before and I don't feel equal to dealing with it if you are going to be silly. Besides, I'm worried about Bill. I think one of us ought to be bathing his head or something . . . it seems frightfully hard-hearted to leave him alone."

Annette, who had shown cold-blooded interest and great excitement over a possible tragedy and was still hanging over the ship's side hoping for something more to happen suddenly realised that other excitements were in store for her and she came shrieking back and offered to show the guests their sleeping quarters.

"But can't we sleep on deck?" enquired Jacky, hoping to avoid more complications about foreign ideas of fresh air.

"That would not be very amusing," answered Annette. "My mamma says the night air has dangers."

The *Hesperus* was now pursuing her course with Captain Brun at the wheel and behind them sailed *La Belle Dame* in the charge of the man left aboard her, and below, knocked out unconscious lay Mr. Bill Briggs. This sad thought much depressed his old crew and once again Jacky marched boldly up to the Skipper and said she thought they should be with him.

"*Mais, non, mademoiselle* . . . a broken head is better quiet, I assure you."

"I *do* feel sorry for Mr. Briggs . . . really I do," wailed Felicity, "but I feel sorry for myself, too, my legs are so cold in this breeze and I *do* wish we were on the other ship."

This was the last straw to Jacky who now noticed that the wind was freshening and that Felicity in a very short cotton skirt was beginning to look a little blue. So far she had not complained of sea-sickness in spite of a rougher sea, but she was now beginning to show signs of the even more severe illness of home sickness. Felicity might be the daughter of a mother who admired Spartan ways, but she was delicate and had always been a spoilt child.

"Now there, Felicity, don't begin to wail. We've all got to take this like sportsmen." Jacky spoke briskly but kindly and Jerry murmured, "I always knew it was a mistake bringing that spoilt brat."

"I'm *frightfully* hungry," announced Bert. "It sounds unsympathetic to say so, I know, but I really could eat the ship. Do you suppose the French ever have tea?"

"Never," said Jacky cruelly. "They miss it out because they eat about twenty times as much as we do in the middle of the day."

It was as if the Skipper guessed their thoughts for he called to Annette—who had gone below to enjoy the rest of the chocolate creams in a nice stuffy atmosphere, and spoke to her and she came running back to her guests.

"Is it you wish for the five o'clock?"

Instantly guessing that they were being asked if they felt like a cup of tea and anxious her charges should be fed Jacky said gratefully, "Oh, Annette, we should *love* it. May we come and help make it?"

"*Oui, oui!*" Annette rushed below followed by the company.

By this time the sky had become speckled with masses

of cloud and the wind was squally and almost chilly and Felicity's legs were not the only ones to feel cold and all *La Belle Dame* crew wore the short woollen cardigans Jacky had insisted upon their bringing. The galley was not in such ship-shape order as the yacht's but to the girls' relief there seemed no fear of starvation for quite an exciting amount of food was stored in the cupboards. The sailor who had rowed them over came down and put on a kettle; but Annette ordered him aft and got out a tin of China tea, a very large thick slab of French chocolate and some long French rolls which she broke into pieces and offered the guests to eat with the chocolate. She would have made "the five o'clock" before the kettle boiled if Jacky had not tactfully suggested boiled water was the English way and they preferred it. It was made and served with dollops of sweet condensed milk and the girls sat round on the red plush seats which was warm, but also decidedly fuggy.

They were grateful to Annette and tried to feel fonder of her.

"Aren't you going to take your father some tea?" asked Jacky.

"*Là! là!*" shrieked Annette. "*Mais, non mademoiselle, il n'est pas un malade, mon Papa!*"

"Oh dear," exclaimed Jerry. "What does she say *now*, Jack?"

"She says her Papa does not drink tea as he is not an invalid. The French only drink tea when they feel ill, or have a cold coming on or something."

"Gracious! Did she offer us tea because she thought we were all sickening for influenza, then?" demanded Georgie.

"Probably she does . . . that's why she finds us so amusing."

"I think I *am*," wailed Felicity. "My head is burning hot and my feet are icy cold and I'm not absolutely sure but I *think* I've got a sore throat."

Felicity, who had seemed so well at Rainbow End was plainly still too nervy and delicate to stand adventures on the sea and Jacky, in despair, felt it was all her fault and never would the dear old Professor and Mrs. Bly call her "a girl of resource" again.

"Oh, Felicity, darling . . . *don't* imagine things. You'll feel quite different after this hot tea and chocolate. Perhaps you had better not go on deck again in this wind. I'll stay, too, and read to you, and perhaps Annette can lend you something warmer to wear."

Annette was delighted to share her wardrobe and gave Felicity the choice of a green velvet coat or a bright pink woollen cardigan. She routed out a book, too, but it was in French and Jacky felt too much worried to translate it.

Tired of Annette's chatter and the stuffy cabin the three girls went above again leaving Jacky to amuse Felicity and delve further into a locker for more warm garments for her.

But on deck the others found the weather had changed and the beautiful blue of the sea had turned to a dirty grey and the ship lifted herself skew-wise over high waves and then plunged with a resounding smack into the trough which was no longer pleasant; in fact, especially after Annette's high tea of chocolate, it made one feel squeamish.

Afraid that Captain Brun would speak French to them and not feeling equal to his broken English they

descended into the cabin again and Annette, at once
noticing they all looked rather green delightedly prophesied an approaching attack of *mal de mer*, and advised
them to recline on the red plush cushions. Jacky played
draughts with the two younger children, glancing every
now and then with dismay at the heaving grey sea
through the port-holes flicked with foam-caps, and
the others groaned and drew horrid pictures of the
scene at Rainbow End when their guardians realised
that they had disappeared.

Hours seemed to pass before they heard a voice above
shouting, " *Mesdemoiselles ! Mesdemoiselles ! La côte
de la France!*"

They rushed on deck. Felicity bundled in Annette's
green velvet coat as well as her pink cardigan and with
her bare legs swathed in two purple woollen scarves
found in the locker. Her own mother would never
have known her.

They all stood in the raging wind and gazed at the
Skipper's finger pointing to a mere streak on the
horizon which thy were thrilled to learn was the fair
land of France.

It was an exciting moment, especially to those of the
party who had never been out of England and even
Jacky would have enjoyed it if it had not been for the
thought of Bill and the despairing parents at Rainbow
End. Behind them *La Belle Dame* ploughed the rough
seas bravely and they longed to be on her for even an
unconscious Bill would be better than no Bill at all.

It was now evening and dark clouds scattered across
the sky and squally rain came in spurts. There was an
alarming thud and a green wave swept across the deck
and immediately Jacky swept the company below

though she longed to stay on deck and watch France approach.

If only some miracle would happen. An aeroplane descend and pick them all up and fly homewards, or Bill suddenly appear on deck and carry them back to the yacht. But as neither of these things was likely to happen the only thing was to make the best of a bad job and keep the party down below cheerful. This was a difficult task because, apart from sea-sickness, the sudden change in the weather and the lack of warm clothing had made everyone chilly, uncomfortable and inclined to quarrel.

Annette, cosy in her tartan frock, routed in another locker and presented Georgie with a man's reefer coat, Bert with a ragged sweater, Jerry had an oilskin cape which she soon cast off saying she would rather freeze than die from the smell of fishy oilskins. She climbed into a bunk and wrapped herself in a blanket and to Jacky's relief Felicity—still complaining of chills, heats and sore throat—consented to do the same.

The unpleasant motion when the ship rose on the top of a high wave and then descended into a trough affected Jerry and Bert more than the others and they both lay groaning and vowing that if they ever reached dry land they would never, never sail again.

"Then you'll have to stay in France for the rest of your life," said Georgie cheerfully. "So the best thing you can do, my dears, is to forget your pains and get Jack to teach you some French."

Annette, unable to follow their quick speech, now in her turn, began to inquire of Jacky what everyone else had said which was the last straw. The rain was now so heavy that it began to come in through the open port-hole which made Felicity shiver so acutely that Jacky became more alarmed than ever and shut it. This caused groans from the others and purrs of delight from Annette who seemed to bloom in a fuggy atmosphere.

"That finishes it," announced Jerry. I'm going up above and I'll let you know when we get to France."

"*Qu'est-ce qu'elle dit?*" inquired Annette and when Jacky had wearily translated Jerry's remark, she cried, "*Mais non, mademoiselle, maintenant nous mangeons, s'il vous plaît,*" and she proceeded to go to the cupboard and bring out several tins of sardines and an iced cake, which very nearly finished off the invalids.

"Now listen to me Jerry, my lad," said Jacky. "You've got to play the game like everyone else. If you get wet, when do you suppose we can get dry clothes, or dry your wet ones? You'll have to stick it down here and be thankful we have a shelter."

Jerry, feeling too ill to argue merely shut her eyes.

It was becoming darker every moment and looking through the port-hole they could see the streak of land getting nearer and nearer and lights were twinkling on it.

Annette made a hearty meal of sardines and iced cake and Georgie ate a roll, Jerry and Bert refused all refreshment and so did Felicity, and Jacky felt that any food would choke her.

The French sailor came down and banged about in the galley and there was a strong smell of coffee. Jacky went to speak to him and offered to carry coffee to the Skipper while he enjoyed his own below. Regardless of the *entente cordiale*, Felicity and Annette quarrelled over their game of draughts and when Georgie volunteered to play with them in her turn Jacky decided to have a talk with the Skipper. She put on the oilskin cape and made her way over the slippery deck and approached him timidly.

"How long will it be before we get into harbour, Captain Brun?"

"*Pardon, mademoiselle.*"

Jacky repeated the question though she had an idea he had heard it and did not wish to answer.

"It is possible in an hour or more, mademoiselle. Soon I will ask the engine power to speed us up."

"But what about *La Belle Dame*?"

"She will follow, naturally."

"I do wish I knew how Mr. Briggs is now."

"*Tiens!* All is well I assure you." Captain Brun, looked as if broken heads were nothing in comparison with his own troubles and Jacky felt guilty. After all, it was awful for him to have five schoolgirls suddenly landed on him without suitable clothes even and waiting to be warmed and fed.

"Captain Brun . . . I suppose we'll all have to stay aboard to-night?"

"*Non, non* . . . my 'ouse, it is not large, no, but my wife will manage, I assure you, mademoiselle."

"Really we would rather stay on the boat, and I thought we could not land in another country without passports and things?"

"*Pardon, mademoiselle.*" Captain Brun most decidedly did not want to discuss the matter and a heavy wave over the deck and his gloomy expression drove Jacky below again as she had no courage to ask him his plans for their return.

In the cabin she found Jerry and Bert still groaning and the game of draughts abandoned for Felicity wept, too, and refused to be comforted by Georgie. She had now awful thoughts about what was happening at Rainbow End in their absence.

"They'll let Cato get into a snare again and we shan't be there to find him."

"Don't be such a little ass. Cato has learnt his lesson about snares."

"Christopher Columbus will be lost down a rabbit-hole."

"And the hens will fly away and the goats go bathing and drown themselves . . . and Billy Slowboy will go off to join the gipsies! Go on, Jacky . . . it's *your* turn to howl now," teased Georgie.

"Besides, you *would* come," said Jerry.

This brought a fresh outburst and Felicity vowed she was being punished for so cruelly deserting Ethel.

"Well, thank goodness Ethel isn't here. She would be certain to say it was all our faults and she would be sea-sick and get a fly in her eye even if we drifted to the Arctic regions where I don't think they have flies."

"You *are* a comfort George, old chap." said Jacky. "I should simply break down if *you* began to groan."

"Well, don't get down-hearted, my lad. I'll stand by you through thick and thin and if ever we get back to our native land I'll pitch a wonderful yarn of how you gathered us all under your oilskin cape like an old mother hen and saved us from starvation and exposure. Shouldn't be surprised if the Queen gave you the George Medal."

"*Qu'est-ce qu'elles disent?*" enquired Annette; but Jacky ignored her and said in an aside to Georgie:

"The Captain says we shall be in soon, but I can't find out properly what he means to do with us. I'm worried to death about Felicity . . . she vows her throat is definitely sore now.''

''She's much too fond of analysing her feelings, that kid. The cricket cure has not yet been quite complete.''

If it had not been for their great anxiety, both girls would have braved the weather and remained on deck for there was something exciting in the thought that they were approaching a strange country though they had no idea what would happen when they reached it. But they knew their place was near the invalids, who, as the weather became rougher became more and more miserable and lay in the bunks now more sea-sick than home-sick in utter despair.

''Do cheer up, Bert. After all land's in sight.''

''What's the good of that when we shall have to face this again before we get home . . . unless we stay in France for ever. Oh, Jacky, why did we ever let ourselves be landed in this mess?''

''Well, you all longed for adventures and now you are having one you don't like it. Here, let me tuck you up, it's jolly cold and you'll feel better if you get warm.''

''And to think that this morning we were boiling hot! It seems months to me since we left Rainbow End. Oh, I do wish somebody would take away that smelly oilskin cape!''

At this moment, Felicity, who had been dozing, sat up and demanded if they were at home.

''Not yet . . . but do look out of the port-hole and you'll see lights. Won't it be wonderful to be able to say you have been to France?''

''No. I don't want to see France. It makes my

head ache to see people talking French, and I don't
like the things they eat.''

Then Annette, who had been asleep on the red plush
seat, sat up, too, and once again enquired, " *Qu'est-ce
qu'elles disent?*" and then shook her head dolefully at
the sight of the moaners around her and pointing to
Felicity said, "That one—*elle a l'air malade*" which
made Jacky more anxious than ever. "They need
tisane." She opened a cupboard door and brought out
a tin of dried herbs—Jacky, who knew how wise the
French are in the use of herbal medicines, was
delighted.

"Oh, Annette . . . can you really make *tisane?*"

"*Mais, oui,*" and then in rapid French she
explained she must have boiling water and Jacky said
she would go with her to the galley.

"Annette is so kind she is going to make you a lovely
French drink called a *tisane* which will make you feel
better," she explained to Felicity.

"I don't want it . . . it sounds like a sneeze . . .
besides, my throat is too sore to swallow it."

Nevertheless, Jacky and a very important, bustling
Annette staggered into the galley and in spite of the
kettle sliding about on the stove and the dim light from
the swinging lantern managed to make a jugful of the
hot, herbal drink and carry it back to the cabin and
coax the sufferers to swallow it.

"The minute we land in France I'll ask the captain
to send a cable to Rainbow End saying ' All well.'"
Jacky promised Felicity.

"Then you will be telling a lie," replied Felicity.
"I'm *not* well and neither is Roberta or Jerry. I didn't
know you told stories, Jacky."

Annette answered that it was now time to go to bed and brought more blankets out of a locker. She said that she and her Papa often spent the night at sea and she rolled herself up snugly and was soon sound asleep.

Georgie and Jacky tucked up the others as warmly as possible but Jacky, in the old woollen jersey and Georgie shivering in the old reefer jacket shared the watch over them faithfully under the smoky, swinging lantern.

CHAPTER XIII

FRANCE

THE two girls were never likely to forget that night's vigil and their friendship became real and lasting during its trials and vicissitudes. In her strange, wandering life Jacky had endured many hardships and could now face most things, but Georgie's life had been sheltered, and it was only her admiration for Jacky and her determination to be like her that made it possible for her to face the cold, the darkness, and need of sleep and rest. She was also really alarmed at being at sea in such stormy weather and the thud of the waves against the port-holes, the creak of ropes and boards and the voices of the captain and his mate above shouting to each other above the wind gave her a feeling of danger and uncertainty. Jacky, cold too, and not too happy in the storm, suffered more from anxiety for them all than fear, especially for Felicity, who was plainly showing she had not yet sufficiently recovered from her delicacy to endure hardship and was, she felt sure, already really ill with cold, shock, and homesickness for the parents she had never before left. She tossed in her bunk, complained of heat and then cold and threw off all her coverings if Jacky took her eyes off her. Worst of all as the hours passed her mind began to wander and she begged to be put to bed in a place that "kept still."

"I expect she will have pneumonia," said Jacky miserably.

"If she does it won't be *your* fault," Georgie replied. You've done your best and the more I think of it the more surprised I am that Bee ever let her come."

"Who could possibly guess things would turn out like this. If only we could send a message to them . . . they must be nearly out of their minds."

"What do you suppose will happen when we land?"

"Goodness knows . . . the Skipper says he will take us to his home, but I never knew people could land in a foreign country without passports."

"I wonder how poor old Bill is?"

"Out of his mind, too, I should think, if he is conscious."

"He must have been out of his mind all along to risk all this and let us come aboard this ship without him."

"I *do* wish you wouldn't whisper." Jerry woke up from a restless doze and sat up. "Where are we? And why are you both sitting up?"

"We don't know *where* we are . . . and *somebody* has to nurse the sick." Georgie sounded scornful.

"Well, you can be thankful you were not sea-sick."

"You *would* eat all that rich chocolate."

"Oh *do* be quiet." Jerry, no longer able to sit up with a swimming head sank down again.

"I say, Georgie, *do* lie down . . . it's marvellous having you for company but you'll be dead to-morrow."

"And what about you? No, you must leave me alone, I'm practising *Rule I* and trying 'to adopt a manly and gentlemanly attitude towards life in general, never showing feminine weakness, or sentimentality in times of hardship and danger'."

Jacky laughed and said, "And poor Jerry is perhaps remembering *Rule IV* 'unnecessary tongue-wagging is sternly discouraged.' Oh dear, I do wonder what time it is."

Only Georgie had worn a watch and hers had stopped.

"Let's take it in turns to watch Felicity and get a snooze."

"I couldn't sleep a wink . . . but I'll lie down if you will."

They stretched themselves on the plush seats and soon Georgie dozed; but Jacky remained wide awake full of fear for Felicity and the awful problem of what they must face when day came. Jerry and Bert tossed and moaned, but at last Felicity slept heavily under the blankets and Jacky got up softly and went to the port-hole. There were streaks of dawn in the sky and the ship was moving more smoothly.

Then she noticed something rather odd; the twinkling lights of the French port that she had watched approach the night before were now in the distance and they seemed to be sailing away from them.

She called Georgie and pointed this out to her.

"It's jolly queer. Do you suppose he's decided to dump us on some desert island?"

"I wish I knew. I thought I would screw up my

courage and go on deck and ask him if you will hold the fort. Felicity is much quieter now."

"Of course I will; but for goodness' sake wrap yourself up in the smelly cape."

The rain had left off and there was a fresh breeze, but the spray was tempestuous enough to give anyone a wetting and Jacky wrapped herself up in the oilskin and went above.

Captain Brun was still at the helm and in the light of dawn Jacky was struck by his air of extreme exhaustion and something else besides this; a look of anxiety and strain. He, too, must have had an awful night and though Jacky was sorry for him and did not want to add to his worries she felt she must ask about his plans. She glanced behind her across the sea and to her great relief saw in the far distance *La Belle Dame* following the schooner.

"*Bonjour, Capitaine.*"

"*Bonjour, mademoiselle.* You and your friends, is it that they have slept well?"

"Not too well, I'm afraid. You see three of them are seasick and though you and Annette have been so kind we are all a little homesick and very anxious to hear what is to become of us?"

"Oh . . . it is bad to be sick for 'ome . . . and an illness, mademoiselle, all sailors well understand."

"Shall we soon be in port? I do so want to let our friends know we are safe."

"*Vraiment* . . . soon we land at a private wharf near to my 'ouse which will be more *convenable.*" The Skipper then closed his mouth grimly and shook his head when Jacky spoke again, as if too much occupied to talk, and the ship went doggedly on as if it had a personality of its own which was as obstinate and glum as its master's. Jacky felt it was true when Sam Jeans said that ships understood.

The streaks of dawn in the east grew brighter and though the light was still dull and grey and the spray came across the deck in sheets, Jacky huddled herself near the roof of the cabin, determined to ignore the taciturn Skipper and watch.

They were entering a little waterway or indentation, too wide for a creek and winding at first and then almost straight with a rough landing place in the distance. To Jacky's great relief the Skipper made for this place and then came a surprise, too, for in the still dim light she saw a group of waiting men.

The Skipper gave a quick order to drop anchor and in a few minutes the *Hesperus* was anchored in the waterway with a distance of about two hundred yards between her and the landing-stage.

"Captain Brun," began Jacky, but she got no further for his white, tense face alarmed her and she felt a queer feeling of approaching disaster.

"*Mon Dieu!*" muttered the Skipper, and his mate cried, "*Voilà les douaniers!*"

Almost in an instant a boat pushed off with three men aboard and it was then that Jacky noticed that two of them wore uniform and the third was in plain clothes. They came alongside rapidly and an order was called out in French that they wished to board the schooner. Jacky sat perfectly still and neither she nor the Skipper spoke one word as the men came aboard and one of them approached Captain Brun and said:

"Monsieur Brun, I arrest you in the name of the Republic."

CHAPTER XIV

INTERROGATION

Before uttering one word of protest to the official, Captain Brun turned to Jacky and hissed, "Mademoiselle, I entreat you to go below . . . all will be well, I assure you, I am a man of honour."

Jacky felt that this was an order to be obeyed and she fled to the cabin.

"What on earth is the matter now? You look as green as Jerry and Bert."

"Oh, Georgie . . . something awful has happened, but please be quiet or everyone will wake up and I simply can't stand having to tell the French what the English say and the English what the French say just yet. Listen . . ." she spoke in a whisper. "Three men have just boarded the boat and arrested the Skipper and the ship and us, too, I suppose, though goodness knows what we've done."

"It can't be true!"

"Yes, it is—hush! They are all waking up."

The invalids were indeed waking with fresh complaints of cold, hunger, thirst and discomfort, in fact of their own special miseries.

"Haven't you and Georgie been to bed at all?" Jerry suddenly felt her conscience prick.

"How could we? You've got all the bunks and all the blankets and Felicity is what Annette calls *une pauvre malade.*"

Jerry struggled up, groaned as her head swam and said,

"I'm sorry I've been such a slacker, but I do feel so awful . . . but I'll have a go with Felicity now."

But Felicity still slept and she now looked so pale that Jacky hoped the feverishness had left her.

Annette, hearing voices, sat up, yawned and then said,

"*Bonjour, mesdemoiselles,*" with her usual politeness. She then rose, ran to the port-hole and cried, "*Bonne chance! Le temps est beau!* And now let us eat, if you please." She seemed quite unconcerned about her Papa's night in the storm and was not curious about his present whereabouts.

This astonished Jacky and Georgie; but the former was so thankful not to have to answer awkward questions. As it happened they had to do this during the next few minutes.

The three men who had boarded the schooner came down into the cabin, showed great surprise to see it full of schoolgirls and one of them said quietly, "*Pardon, mesdemoiselles. Est-ce qu'il y a parmi vous quelqu'un qui parle francais?*"

Jacky with a sigh came forward.

"I speak a little French, monsieur, but it would be easier for me to speak in English."

"*Bien, mademoiselle. Monsieur Kemp, s'il vous plaît.*"

The French official who had spoken turned to the little man in plain clothes who came forward and Jacky sighed with relief. He was so plainly an Englishman and his opening remark gave her instant confidence.

"Now then, missy, don't be afraid. You are all in

safe hands but we shall have to ask you a few questions. Answer them truthfully and briefly and that will make it O.K. for all of us."

"I'll try." Jacky's heart sank again for she felt in her bones that the kind of question asked would be of a nature to get Bill Briggs into trouble.

"Why are you and these young ladies on this boat intending to land in France without passports?"

Jacky explained that she and her friends had been cruising in a friend's yacht and had met the *Hesperus* and visited her. In the meantime the Skipper of the yacht had had an accident.

The officer explained this to the others and they nodded with approval as the tale evidently tallied with the Skipper's.

"What is the name of your yachting friend?"

This was awful, but determined to be truthful Jacky answered, "Mr. William Briggs."

"And do you mean to say that your teachers—I hear you come from a girls' school—allowed you to sail with a stranger?"

"He was not a stranger, he was a friend."

"Humph! A friendly action I must say to get you all in this mess! I hear he's got a broken head which serves him right and also saves him some unpleasantness at the moment. And now what about this schoolmistress . . . she knows nothing of what has happened to you?"

"Oh, no . . . that's the awful part of it and that is her little girl asleep in the bunk and she is really ill. *Please* could you help us to send her a message?"

"That, I will do immediately . . . the address please?"

He took out a note-book and Jacky gave him the address carefully.

"Which is Annette Brun, Monsieur Brun's daughter?"

Annette was pushed forward and told by the officers that her Papa was going ashore and wished her to accompany him.

"La! la! Quelle bonne chance! Mes amies . . . viendront-elles, aussi?"

"Non, non. Allez-y vite! mon enfant."

Annette, her tartan frock crumpled, her curls no longer in corkscrews, like a true Frenchwoman gave a few deft pulls and touches to her garments and vanished up the companion-way with the French officers calling, "Au revoir, mesdemoiselles. A la prochaine!" The English wondered if she would be arrested with her Papa and wished they could have supplied her with some comforting chocolate creams.

"But what is to become of us?" asked Jacky.

"Mademoiselle, you are now in France and without passports. You are what is called 'aliens.' This ship is under observation and will remain at anchor until she has been searched. You must all remain aboard until we can get into touch with your friends."

"What about Mr. Briggs?"

"He is under arrest, too. When his boat anchors— which will be soon, we shall board her, and if he is too ill for interrogation we shall take him to hospital for treatment."

"But what have he and Captain Brun done?"

"Your friend, Mr. Briggs, is a very daring and a very unscrupulous contrabandier, which in English means he is a smuggler."

The girls all pricked up their ears and became madly excited, for, strange to say, even in these days when real adventure has reached the greatest heights smuggling still sounds romantic and remarkable.

"But I didn't know people smuggled now . . . I thought it was only in the eighteenth century." Georgie could not resist taking part in the conversation.

"Not a bit of it. Those old smugglers in the eighteenth century were a lot of picturesque cut-throats who were driven to cheat the revenue because the laws kept them so poor."

"But parsons smuggled too!

Brandy for the parson, baccy for the clerk,
Laces for a lady, letters for a spy,
And watch the wall, my darling, till the gentlemen
go by."

"Oh, yes . . . we all know that other people did it, too, because they enjoyed adventure and it is the same to-day . . . lots of young chaps think it thrilling and daring to smuggle and I must say present-day smugglers have to face greater dangers and must be smarter than the old chaps with brass rings in their ears. It all sounds very romantic but they are just as dishonest and are cheating the Queen's revenue."

Roberta, who, as it has been explained had never really thirsted for adventure and certainly did not look like a bold modern smuggler at the present moment sat up weakly and said:

"I say, please, will *we* be arrested?"

"Cheer up . . . we'll keep you out of gaol if we can!

Now I must be off and get your message sent. Stay where you are till I return. Is there enough food?''

"Tons."

"Well, so long . . . and be good."

"May we go on deck?"

"Go where you like, so long as you don't escape or fall overboard. I should keep below until we've got your good friend, Mr. Briggs, where he ought to be."

"Will he go to prison?"

"It depends on the magistrate . . . if we can't stop all this smuggling by giving heavy fines we'll have to see what prison does . . . now I must go."

He departed and Jacky gave a sigh of relief. "Wasn't it marvellous he could speak English? To think if he hadn't I should have to have told you all that! And he's so kind, too. I feel that he will get that message off soon."

Felicity, who had actually slept soundly through it all, now sat up and demanded to know why the boat was not moving and where the "horrid little French girl" had disappeared to; and wasn't there something to drink that didn't taste like scent?

"Never mind, pet . . . the scented drink did you no end of good and Annette was really a kind little girl and you would have been frozen without her clothes. She's gone now and we have this ship all to ourselves until they come and take us back to England . . . won't it be fun?"

"Have you told Mummy and Dad how ill I am?"

"You are not ill now . . . but you must stay where you are and keep warm to be quite safe. I'll open the port-hole for you to get more air and you shall have your breakfast 'in bunk'."

" What will it be? My clothes are *so* uncomfortable, Jacky."

" Oh, for goodness' sake, stop grousing, child," cried Georgie. " You are like that thing they talk about on the wireless, 'a little Depression from Iceland,' and we are all sick of it. Don't you realise Jacky has been up all night with you?"

This rather silenced Felicity and she lay quietly while they trooped into the galley and lit the oil-stove. Jacky found oatmeal, tinned milk and tea and flour and decided to make an Irish loaf as the bread had all been eaten.

The sun was shining again and if it had not been for the uncertainty of the future it was rather fun having the *Hesperus* to themselves; even if she was under arrest and they themselves were called "aliens."

While Jacky mixed her bread, Georgie lowered a pail by a rope into the water and they all had a wash which refreshed the seasick Jerry and Bert. They took off their frocks and shook them and Georgie suggested they could have a washing-day and dry them on deck; but Jacky said it would never do if the Custom officers returned while they were in their petticoats.

When breakfast was ready the three girls carried their's on deck while Jacky stayed with *la petite malade* who said now that everything tasted " fishy."

Jerry and Bert, now quite recovered, washed up while Georgie swabbed the deck. Felicity now demanded to get up and do some swabbing, too, in spite of her avowal that she was still very ill. A shout from the deck made Jacky leave her and rush to join the others and she found them all eagerly watching a steam-launch coming from the direction of the sea-port.

"I believe it's coming here—more policemen, perhaps."

"So long as it isn't any more 'interrogation.' I'm so afraid of getting poor Bill into more trouble."

"Oh look . . . *La Belle Dame* is coming in!"

La Belle Dame was slowly entering the straight stretch of the waterway and as the girls watched eagerly she dropped anchor. The steam-launch drew alongside and evidently called for a ladder because Jacques appeared and lowered one. There were three people in the boat, a man with a bag, evidently a doctor, a nurse, and an official in uniform. It seemed ages before they appeared on deck again and then they were carrying a stretcher on which lay a form wrapped in blankets and this was lowered carefully into the boat.

"Oh poor Bill . . . he must be worse!"

"And to think there's nobody he knows on the yacht. *We* ought to be imprisoned on an English boat, not a French one."

Jacques went on to the launch, too, and was evidently under arrest and the launch began its noisy journey back to the port leaving *La Belle Dame* deserted. It was a sad sight, and made them feel more homesick than ever, in fact Jacky saw at once that the prisoners must be kept occupied to keep cheerful.

"We are jolly lucky having plenty of food," she said. "I never saw such a lot of tins. It looks as if the Skipper expected to land on a desert island. But if you are all going to eat as much as you did at breakfast we shall need them. What shall we have for dinner?"

Felicity, of course, said she could only eat ice-cream and the others vowed they couldn't bear to think of tinned meats on so hot a day.

"Well, when in Rome we are told to do as the Romans do, so when in France let's do what the French do and have *hors d' œuvres*."

But Jerry said this reminded her too much of Annette's sardines and Bert said she fancied macaroni with tomatoes.

"That's a good idea. I remember now seeing packets of macaroni and tins of tomato juice in the cabin." Jacky went to the cupboard over one of the lockers which was stacked with tins and packets and reached up for a long packet marked *macaroni Italienne*.

She cut off the sealed top with a knife and *a shower of cigars fell on the table*.

They all stood staring at them for a few moments and then Georgie said, "Gosh! Then the Skipper *is* a smuggler!"

"What on earth shall we do with them?"

"If we throw them overboard they'll float on the sea and the Custom men will think we are aiding and abetting and they'll say *we* are smugglers."

"I suppose we are."

"What on earth do you mean, Jack?"

"Hush—don't let Felicity hear . . . but don't you remember those heavy knapsacks we took to 'The Jolly Mariners'?"

"I say, rather. What on earth will the Professor and Bee say?"

"I think Bill is a *beast*. Fancy landing us into all

this!" Roberta, with no wish for adventure, was indignant.

"You jolly well enjoyed the smugglers' tea."

"I always thought there was something fishy about that squid."

"I suppose John Lillywhite is a smuggler, too. Oh, I do hope Sam and Mrs. Jeans are not smugglers . . . it would spoil everything so!"

Jacky put the cigars back in the packet and replaced it on the shelf and said she absolutely refused to be "interrogated" about them.

"But now the macaroni has turned into cigars . . . what shall we eat?"

"Nothing out of this cupboard . . . let's try the fruit tins in the galley."

They opened them in fear and trembling; but the innocent-looking tins turned out to be really innocent and they made their meal of fruit and bread and butter and large cups of tea.

Felicity, who had slept off and on all morning now woke up and complained that the cabin was suffocating.

"The port-holes are all open . . . do look at the lovely, calm sea, Felicity, and oh, I say, there's another launch and it's coming *here!*"

It was quite true that a noisy little launch was approaching the *Hesperus*—as it drew nearer to the amazement and great joy of the watchers Professor Bly and Mrs. Bly were in it with the English Customs officer and a French one. Leaving Jacky to calm the excited Felicity, and it was as much as she could do to keep her under the blankets, the others rushed on deck.

"Oh Jacky, *do* let me go, too. I promise I'll wind

those awful purple scarves of Annette's round my legs. Won't it make Mummy's heart ache to see me with no warm clothes?''

''Don't be so babyish, Felicity. We were *all* cold, and you had most of the blankets. Why can't you be a little sport?''

''I'm too ill . . . you have to feel well to be a sport.''

''Then if you are so ill, lie still, for goodness' sake.''

Cheers from above made Jacky rush to the port-hole to see the launch now alongside and the Professor was waving his hand and Mrs. Bly was anxiously scanning the deck for her precious child. The first thing she shouted was, ''Where are Felicity and Jacintha?''

''In the cabin . . . all safe!'' yelled Georgie.

By now quite adept seamen, they managed to lower the ladder and the party boarded the ship. Mrs. Bly gave her pupils one rapid glance, saw they were crumpled and much the worse for wear but intact and then she said briefly, ''You have very nearly killed me, girls . . . take me to this cabin.''

The officers stayed on deck and the others went below for the re-union, which was particularly affecting between the parents and their only child.

''Jacky saved my life, Mummy,'' announced Felicity. ''I think I was dying; but she sat up all night and gave me horrid scented drinks and held the bed-clothes on me. A beastly little French girl was here, too, and she would offer us chocolate creams when we felt seasick, but she lent me these awful scarves to wrap round my legs because I nearly froze, didn't I Jacky?''

''My precious!'' Mrs. Bly hugged her ewe lamb and holding out her hand to Jacky drew her close saying, "Oh, Jacintha . . . how can we ever thank you?"

"But I didn't do anything but try to keep her warm. I think she is all right now, really, but I was afraid to let her get up." Jacky's relief was so great that she felt a warm glow inside and out; for she had felt so strongly that she would be blamed for letting them leave the yacht to visit the schooner.

The Professor, too, wrung her hand and said, "Good girl . . . all through these anxious hours we have comforted ourselves with the thought that you were in charge and common sense would prevail."

Bursting with relief and pride, but feeling all praise was undeserved, Jacky said: "Georgie has been wonderful. I couldn't have done without her help," and then feeling sorry for the rest of the "boys" in her brigade, she added, "Poor Jerry and Roberta were seasick," and they gave her a glance of gratitude.

"How much do you know about it all, please?" asked Jacky.

"A great deal more than we feel able to bear," the Professor looked solemn. "The English interpreter has done his best, poor chap, to make it all sound very innocent, but it's a nice position for a respectable school-master to find his pupils are mixed up with a gang of smugglers!"

"Oh, Professor, I know! But really and truly we had no idea!"

"Papa . . . how soon are we going home?" demanded Felicity. "And how are Ethel and Cato and Christopher Columbus?"

"All well, my love, and we shall go home the moment they will let us. But somebody—and it must be

Jacintha, as the eldest and most sensible, has to accompany these two gentlemen to the Customs for what they call 'a little interrogation'."

"Oh dear! But they have already asked me hundreds of questions . . . and ought I to tell them all Bill's secrets?"

"You certainly ought . . . *fiat justitia ruat cœlum* . . . which you all ought to know means let justice be done though the heavens are falling."

"Oh, don't talk Latin to them now, please Jim, and I'm sure Jacintha doesn't want to do too much harm to poor Mr. Briggs. Nobody can say he wasn't a nice young man, though I find it hard to forgive what he has done to us."

"The question is, my dear, will the Queen forgive him? He has been robbing the revenue quite a long time, I believe. But now I must join the officers of the law who are impatient to get to their job and search the ship though they are too polite to say so while all you ladies are on board."

Jacky looked at the others and then said, "Oh, please, Professor and Mrs. Bly, we are frightfully sorry we have been such a worry," and the others added sheepishly, "*Awful* for you . . . and you must have been desperate about Felicity."

"I was desperate about you *all*," said Mrs. Bly briskly. "And I'm quite sure you are all sorry and as somebody once said all adventures begin by running away from home I suppose you are now adventurers."

"But we didn't run away . . . Bill ran away with us!"

"And we can be sure he will offer some explanation

. . . come along, Jacintha . . . goodbye, my dear, we'll be back as soon as possible."

Jacky found she was to be taken in the launch to the Customs for her interrogation and she wished she looked less awful and her hair less like a lot of rats' tails full of salt from the spray.

The launch travelled quickly and strange to say the Professor did not say a word to the officers about their errand but talked about prehistoric man, cricket and the convenience of a Channel tunnel, etc., and this, Jacky found, made her feel much less nervous. They were taken to a building on the wharf and led into an office where an important looking official sat at a table.

"This is the young lady, sir."

Jacky's knees began to shake again, but to her relief the official smiled and said in English, "Do not be alarmed, mademoiselle, but just answer the questions very carefully. How did you first meet Mr. William Briggs?"

"At Mrs. Jeans' cottage. She cooks for the school. Oh, please, don't say Mr. Jeans is a smuggler?"

"That's what we want to find out. Did this Mr. Briggs ever ask you to carry messages or packets anywhere?"

Jacky hesitated and the Professor said, "The whole story, Jacintha, please, and remember you are doing your best for Briggs and everyone concerned."

"Well, on the day we first met him he asked us to take a message to the farmer, Mr. Farley."

"Do you remember the message?"

Jacky repeated it and the officers looked at one another.

"What sort of man is this Farley?"

"He's just a Dorset farmer and he's a grandson who plays a good game of cricket," put in the Professor.

"A pity he doesn't play cricket himself instead of smuggling cigars and hiding them in his hayricks."

Jacky gave a start and remembered Bill's message. "Tell him I'll be round to give a hand with the ricks."

"Did Briggs ever ask you to carry anything else besides messages?"

"Yes . . . but it was only a game because we wanted to have an adventure . . . at least the girls did. Mr. Briggs invented an adventure for us and pretended we were in the Secret Service."

"Where did you go?"

Jacky described The Jolly Mariner and this caused almost a sensation; in fact the men seemed so delighted she rather timidly asked why they were pleased.

"We've been on the scent of that place for nearly two years but could never get any real clue though we knew pretty well that somebody there was smuggling brandy and tobacco. What sort of packets were they?"

"Just knapsacks . . . he said they were secret despatches."

"And you believed him?"

"No . . . I thought it was a game . . . but the others believed it. They gave us a gorgeous tea at the Inn."

"Have you ever seen anything like this on the yacht?"

The official nodded to an attendant and he fetched some tins gaily labelled and inscribed *Tomato Juice, Superfine.*

Jacky shook her head. "No, he had ham and cherries and cake but no tomato juice."

"Open one, Doncet."

The attendant took up a tin-opener and prised open the tin carefully and handed it to the official who gently turned the contents upside down on the table; a closely packed assortment of beautiful little Swiss watches, some of them jewelled.

"A nice little lot," he said grimly. "Mr. Bill Briggs must have done well out of imported tomato juice. We've been watching for these tinned luxuries a long time, haven't we, Mr. Kemp?"

"That's right, sir. The last one we saw was labelled *Homard Italien* . . . but it must have been a hard lobster to digest. All very ingenious with the maker's name on the label, which shows there are plenty of clever people in this racket."

"Do you mean to say Mr. Briggs smuggled these watches?"

"They were in his yacht, miss—handed over by Monsieur Brun we imagine and he was clever enough, too, to take out a nice innocent little party of school-girls to do some of his dirty work for him."

"What will they do to him?"

"Mend his head first . . . then see what he has to say for himself. It's my belief he's mixed up with a gang of young men who are doing this more for the thrill and adventure than any love of gain, though he's spent plenty on that yacht of his and has had a good time on the Continent with his friends."

"Who is Captain Brun, please . . . he was kind?"

"He's a respectable tradesman who owns a boat, too, and thought he would make some extra money by handling contraband goods in mid-channel to your friend. All very innocent . . . little daughter aboard and all that. Now that is all, mademoiselle. We have got these men and I congratulate you on your clear and sensible way of answering questions. Monsieur, the launch will take you back to your friends and you may leave for England any time. I thank you."

Everyone shook hands and they were free to depart and in spite of Jacky's relief she could not help saying, "Oh, poor Bill!"

CHAPTER XV

THE BOYS BECOME GIRLS AGAIN

It must have been the nice English interpreter who pulled all the strings because it was arranged that they were to fly home to England, travelling by launch to the French seaport and then taking a taxi to the aerodrome.

"So we shall *land* in France!"

"I think we ought to call on Annette and return her purple scarves—jolly useful they were as stockings."

"I wonder if she will ever sail in the *Hesperus* again."

"I wonder if she ever opened a tin of Swiss watches in mistake for sardines."

Everyone was in the wildest spirits and even Felicity left off issuing bulletins of her health when she heard she was actually going to fly.

Mrs. Bly, who had now been told all about the secret despatches adventure and was now aghast, listening to everyone making excuses for Bill Briggs because he had only done it to "make them enjoy themselves."

"But why on earth did you want adventure, girls? I am sure things were never dull for you at Rainbow End."

"Well you see . . ." Jacky looked desperate, but was determined to make a clean breast of it, "I got up a sort of secret society called the Boys' Brigade."

"Oh, Jacintha . . . *not* a secret society in *my* school! So silly and so schoolgirlish!"

"I tried not to make it silly and schoolgirlish and one rule was that we had to learn some craft and we told Bill and he suggested sailing."

"It wasn't a bit silly . . . really it wasn't, Mrs. Bly." Georgie was indignant.

"Well it sounds *very* silly to me and not a bit what I expected from my girls and I don't want to hear any more about it . . . especially when I think it led to all this."

"Adventures are for the adventurous, my dear," put in the Professor. "And ships are safe in harbour, but we all know that that wasn't why ships were built. This adventure won't make them silly, but wary, for as Horace says, 'guard oneself as one may, every moment is an ambush.' I suppose all these young men have enjoyed the adventurous part of smuggling and boys will be boys, though I agree with you that we mustn't encourage *girls* to be boys, which seems to be the reason for Jacintha's secret society."

"I should think not indeed."

"All the same, I hear they are not the only young lady smugglers. The Customs officer told me that not very long ago another young lady, who happened to have a false eye, smuggled a diamond worth £15,000 at the back of it."

"Jolly useful to have a false eye if you enjoy smuggling," remarked Jerry.

"And now here's the launch waiting, and we can leave the sea for the air . . . has everybody got everything?"

But all the belongings they had were their cardigans which were as crumpled as their frocks and Mrs. Bly said she was ashamed of appearing with such a shabby-looking party on a smart aeroplane.

All they saw of France were the docks of the port and the gesticulating French people seeing off their nice, safe friends and relations in nice, safe steamers with no contraband goods aboard.

When they reached the gates of the aerodrome planes were whirling overhead like gigantic birds and Felicity announced she would rather go home by train, please, and Roberta disgraced the B.B. by asking the man at the gate if it was really safe weather for flying.

They were conducted across a field where an aeroplane rested. It looked huge, and the propellers were already vibrating. Felicity needed great encouragement to go up the ladder which led into the cabin, and she was not made any happier when she was fastened in her seat. Jacky, in the role of chief-comforter, sat behind her and Georgie, to her delight, had a seat beside a window. A charming air hostess came round with cotton-wool and advised them to plug their ears to deaden the noise of the engines. Then, came the exciting moment when the pilot climbed aboard, the cabin door was bolted, the propellers whirled, and the roar of the plane proclaimed they were moving. First, the plane taxied along the ground, and then there was a bumping noise and they were mounting up, up, and were actually flying.

Everyone who has flown knows how different this is from travelling in the fastest express-train. No rushing past trees, fields and hedges, but flying through the air with all the scenery of towns, houses and country beneath them.

A magic carpet come true! It was disagreeable when the plane dropped a few hundred feet, and Felicity clutched Jacky and said she *knew* it was dropping down and would bump the earth. But in a minute it had righted itself and travelled upwards again, swept through a bank of cloud and then emerged into sunlight.

On they flew over a patchwork of fields, rivers, villages. Then they were over the Channel where the cross-channel steamers looked very small and unexciting and seemed to move like snails. Nobody could hear what anyone else said which to Jacky was a relief. All the same, it was funny to see Georgie—always talkative —open her mouth and shut it again like a wooden puppet, for nobody had any idea what she said.

"Dover Castle!" shouted the Professor at last— though nobody heard him—and almost immediately they were flying over their native land again and were soon scrambling down the steel ladder into England.

"How lovely not to hear that shrieking French," said Felicity who was no fonder of adventures in foreign lands than Roberta.

More taxis to the station. A wash and a meal at the restaurant there, and then came the train to take them back to the camp.

Telegrams had been sent and when they reached

Rainbow End at dusk they found everyone out on the dancing green waving small Union Jacks. Doris was waving a tea-towel, too, and yes, there was Mrs. Jeans, wearing her man's cap holding Cato in her arms. They felt absolutely certain she was not a smuggler, but a nice, safe country body with a light hand for "puddins."

There was much excitement and plenty of questions, but the girls had been warned to say nothing about the smuggling until more was known about Bill Briggs for as the Professor said, "every man is innocent until he is proved guilty."

Ethel Forbes, always before nicknamed "Ethelred, the Unready" by Miss Lyle, now proved herself ready for all emergencies and wearing a paper Red Cross apron and cap she had had in a birthday party cracker, at once established herself as chief nurse. The prodigals were given hot baths, had the salt washed out of their hair and were put to bed for supper which consisted of some of Mrs. Jeans' famous chicken jelly soup which she vowed was so strong and nourishing it "stood up by itself."

They slept like tops and in the morning rather enjoyed telling everyone else about Bill's accident, the storm at sea and the *Hesperus* and its French crew.

"And how did you get on with the French girl?" Miss Lyle asked hopefully.

"You had better ask Jacky that, Miss Lyle," Georgie grinned and Jacky groaned.

Three days passed and then another shock shook the peaceful inhabitants of Broomy Hill when one fine morning the daily papers appeared with startling head-lines: *AERIAL AND YACHT SMUGGLING IN THE*

*CHANNEL!   YOUNG   ENGLISHMEN   AND
FRENCHMEN INVOLVED!*

*Following investigations over many months, ending
recently in a raid on a privately-owned yacht, one of
the most remarkable prosecutions for smuggling will
shortly be heard,* etc. etc.

There were portraits of Bill Briggs and Monsieur
Brun and yes, there was one of John Lillywhite, too!

"Thank goodness there isn't one of Sam Jeans and
Mrs. Jeans," said Jacky.

"Rather thank goodness there is not one of Jacintha
Drew, Georgina, Jerry and Roberta," added Mrs. Bly
severely. "We are lucky to have escaped *that*
disgrace!"

The papers said that Bill Briggs was one of a notorious smuggling gang who had been making a good thing
of illegal traffic in tobacco, brandy, and perfumes, and
watches for nearly two years. He worked with the
Frenchman, Monsieur Brun, who was not a Captain at
all, but a respectable chemist. A great deal of the
smuggled stuff had been sold to John Lillywhite. One
member of the gang, who was in the Air Force had
actually jettisoned cigars from his plane into Farley's
field where they had been hidden in hay-ricks until
they could be distributed.

Bill Briggs worked in his father's office and was a
spoilt, only son so he had plenty of time on his hands
to sail his yacht and enjoy being a smuggler.

The aerial smuggling had been very ingenious. After
a strict watch had been kept by the Customs and
Revenue men along the coast and at airports, suspicion
was aroused when cigars were found on the beach near
Farley's farm wrapped in water-proof paper. They

were believed to have been intended for the "ricks."

"And I bet you old Billy Slowboy was turned into a smuggler the night he was borrowed," cried Jacky, recalling the time Bill took away her innocent donkey and afterwards sent her those magnificent chocolates.

"Oh, dear, I wonder what will happen to Bill. I do wish I could have 'turned my face to the wall, my darling, when *that* gentleman went by'."

"He didn't care what happened to *us* when he sent us to The Jolly Mariners." Roberta was still indignant.

"Do you remember the naval man who asked us where we were hiking . . . I suppose *he* was an Excise officer."

"And I bet the deaf and dumb man was a smuggler."

Broomy Hill was all agog for news and on the whole felt indignant that their rural village should have become notorious as a rendezvous for smugglers. As for Sam Jeans and Mrs. Jeans—Bill's special friends— they could not believe their ears.

"Me and Sam—us do be completely flabbergasted, sir," Mrs. Jeans said twenty times a day to the Professor.

To everyone's great relief the Boys' Brigade's part in the affair was entirely kept out of the news and it was constantly impressed upon them how thankful they ought to be for this.

Jacky *was* thankful; but Georgie and Jerry would rather have enjoyed having their photographs in the papers.

Then came the day when Mr. Bill Briggs, recovered from his concussion, appeared in court before the magistrate and summoned for evading custom duties on certain articles, and made a clean breast of the whole thing. He vowed that neither he or his friends had any commercial interest in it and all the smuggling was done in the spirit of adventure and he much regretted it had caused trouble to so many people. The magistrate spoke to him very severely and said the country must be protected from such unlawful deeds and that he was much inclined to make an example of him by sending him to prison. However, he would give him another chance and let him off with a heavy fine. Monsieur Brun, Farmer Farley, and John Lillywhite, were heavily fined, too, and the latter was no longer to be allowed to sell "Spirits and Tobacco," but would have to entertain any Jolly Mariners that visited him with lobster teas and a view of the squid.

Bill Briggs wrote a handsome letter of apology to Rainbow End. He told them *La Belle Dame* and his car would have to be sold to help pay the fines; but he hoped that some happy day would come when he would be forgiven and be invited to play a game of cricket again with the school team.

"I always said he was a nice young man." Mrs. Bly forgave him then and there for Felicity was quite recovered and was even enjoying boasting about her visit to France to Ethel Forbes, and the rest of the amateur smugglers were properly penitent and taking a real interest in folk-dancing.

When the excitement of the case was over Jacky was invited to visit the Professor's wigwam one day where Mrs. Bly was awaiting her and she was told they wished to thank her once again for the way she had dealt with a very serious situation, and especially the way she had kept Felicity from illness and danger.

"But it was all my fault," said Jacky, happy in their praise, but miserable when she remembered that it was the B.B. that had really started it all.

"*Your* fault! . . . My dear child!"

"Well, you know *I* did start it all in a way. I did so want the girls to like me and Georgie was so awfully nice to me the night I came and she was so keen on having a secret society. I knew it was silly, and I hated the idea really, but I *did* start it and make the rules which led to all this."

"Well, so long as you are repentant and promise—as Bill Briggs has—never to do it again and suppress your secret society just as he has suppressed his smuggling pursuits we will forget all about it."

"I'll never have a secret society again, I promise you. If I get up anything I'll call it The Good Girls' Guild, or something and teach them nothing but cooking."

"Good girl . . . that would be splendid, and just what they need. Now listen to our plan . . . are you happy with us?"

"Oh yes, *frightfully* happy now."

"Then we want you to stay with us always—if your step-father will consent—and be our elder daughter and Felicity's sister and help us in the school. There is a little room at the very top of our house in Hampstead and you can have it for your very own and hang your lovely prints there until you can hang them in a home of your own."

"Oh, Professor . . . Mrs. Bly . . . do you really mean you *want* me?"

"Why . . . we can't do without you . . . Felicity

adores you and haven't we always said you are a girl
of resource and just what the school needs?"

"*Juncta juvant* . . . united we assist each other,"
said the Professor and kissed his new daughter.

CHAPTER XVI

WHERE THE RAINBOW ENDS

THERE was much going on one late September day at
Rainbow End and the scene on the dancing-green
looked like a gay, coloured print. Girls, so sunburnt
and hardy that they still wore summer frocks although
there was an autumn tang in the air, were folding up
the bright-hued blankets, and bed-covers and household linens they had used in the camp-school during
the summer. Jacky, and her then special friends, were
packing up their tent and the Professor gave them
advice about the way to do it as he polished up Griselda's
harness. Mrs. Jeans and Doris were sorting out pots
and pans and Doris was no longer a pale little Cockney,
but as brown as a berry and most reluctant to leave the
country where she had learnt so much about sparrows
and nightingales. Mrs. Bly, Miss Lyle and Miss Carroll
were packing suitcases and Felicity and Ethel Forbes
were giving Cato and Christopher Columbus a last run.
Cato now thought the country mouse much more exciting that the town one and Christopher Columbus had
made many discoveries among the rabbit-warrens.

"I'm glad Sam and Mrs. Jeans are going to take on
Smuggler Slowboy and the goats and hens till next

summer," said Jacky. "They will do everything we do for them and are sure to make them comfortable."

"And Mrs. Jeans says they are glad to do it as there's not much in beach-combing when you find nothing but Woolworth's brooches and false teeth."

"Which makes it all the more honest of them not to have joined the smugglers." Roberta still disapproved of Bill.

"I *do* wish we were going to bicycle home . . . it was such fun when we came." Jerry didn't like sitting still.

"I don't think we had any real fun till Jacky turned up," replied Georgie loyally, "and don't forget Jacky you are going to spend part of the Christmas hols with us if the Blys can spare you."

"Thanks awfully . . . I'd love it."

"Girls," called Miss Lyle. "Come to your meal now—the cars will be here in an hour."

All that were left of the school's pupils, for those who had gone home for the holidays were to rejoin them in London, sat down to their last picnic meal at the top of the cliff before changing into travelling-clothes and making one more rush to the shore to say goodbye to the sea.

Mrs. Jeans had made dozens of her special little jam-tarts and cheese-cakes as light as the proverbial feather, and Georgie—the ever faithful—said that they were delicious but that their last meal at Rainbow End was not so delicious as their first meal, Lob's Scouse.

"Papa," said Felicity. "We are leaving Rainbow End and we haven't found the treasure. You said we should find the greatest treasure on earth, or you would be a Dutchman."

"Well, my pet, and so we have. When I see all these bouncing lassies all around me as brown as berries, as strong as horses and eating jam-tarts as heartily as ploughboys and notice that your own little skinny arms and legs have become nice and round I should say we have found Health which *is* the greatest treasure on earth."

"But there must be a crock of gold at each end of the rainbow—two treasures:

Where the Rainbow ends as I've been told
Lies treasure hid in a crock of gold!"

chanted Ethel.

"Then Jacky must be the other treasure," exclaimed Felicity, "Isn't it jolly that we found her?"

THE END